The Loosening Skin *is a sensuous, thought provoking meditation on love that deserves not only a second read, but a third as well. This book will cement Aliya Whiteley's reputation as one of the finest of a new generation of weird fiction writers. More, please.*

HELEN MARSHALL, author of *Gifts for the One Who Comes After*

Strange, confounding and satisfyingly original, Whiteley's new novel is an exploration of relationships and the corrosive effect of time. A speculative enquiry into the meaning of freedom itself, The Loosening Skin *will surprise and delight Whiteley's existing readership and new fans equally. Above all, this is a book that will excite intense discussion.*

NINA ALLAN, author of *The Rift* and *The Race*

Aliya Whiteley's fiction simultaneously scintillates with ideas, skips back and forth across genre boundaries with an ease and audacity that is glorious to behold, and retains such a sense of immediacy and emotional integrity that her readers are drawn into her worlds body and soul. She has the enviable ability to explore big ideas in the most intimate of settings, and to create wholly original realities that leap instantly from the page. For me, she is very much at the forefront of the new wave of UK genre writers.

– MARK MORRIS, author of *Toady, Stitch* and many more

Also by Aliya Whiteley
The Beauty
The Arrival of Missives

Also available from Unsung Stories
Déjà Vu by Ian Hocking
Dark Star by Oliver Langmead
Winter by Dan Grace
The Bearer of Grievances by Joseph McKinley
The Speckled God by Marc Joan
The Dancer by Rab Ferguson
Metronome by Oliver Langmead
Pseudotooth by Verity Holloway
You Will Grow Into Them by Malcolm Devlin
2084 edited by George Sandison
This Dreaming Isle edited by Dan Coxon
The Willow By Your Side by Peter Haynes

THE LOOSENING SKIN

SKIN

ALIYA WHITELEY

UNSUNG
STORIES

Published by Unsung Stories

43 Mornington Road, Chingford
London E4 7DT, United Kingdom

www.unsungstories.co.uk

First edition published in 2018
First impression

Paperback ISBN: 978-1-907389-61-0
ePub ISBN: 978-1-907389-62-7

Edited by George Sandison & Dan Coxon

Cover Artwork © Tara Bush 2018

Cover design by Vince Haig
Text design by Cox Design Limited
Typesetting by George Sandison

Printed in the UK by TJ International

FOR CLARE BROWN

PART ONE

2005. PILLS.

Some people burn love and some people bury it. Some keep it locked up, or push it far under the bed. Some sell it.

The awards ceremony is over and Max didn't win.

That is fine with him. 'It wasn't my best work,' he says into the phone, on the drive to Sussex. He sprawls in the back of the limo, beside me. 'I can do better. I want to feel like I earned it. I might try directing.' Then he shrugs, and says, 'Well, yeah, I know. But I can't run away from Daddy's shadow forever.' He has long conversations on the phone with his psychiatrist about his father, and what it means to be a success in a world where money no longer has meaning.

When he puts the phone down I tell him, 'You did deserve it. You just didn't get it. Different things.' We squeeze hands.

Awards. Weights and measures, women and men, prizes and parties and perfection. It's late, and I've watched Max all day in a professional capacity. Now I can watch him in my own time, and he is a sight in that suit, the lines cut sharp over his shoulders, the shirt so white; I want him, and so much more than that. Chemistry is one way of describing it, but underneath that there is love. I don't care what the science books say; love doesn't only have to be as deep as this layer of skin. It can survive. When it feels like this it must survive.

At the house, Max walks ahead of me to the bedroom, and I follow with my eyes on nothing but him. He knows it. He loses the jacket and throws it over the tall Greek vase. He strips the bow tie from around his neck and drapes it on the frame of the Pissarro. The cufflinks he deposits on the neon fish tank. It's a running joke that this estate of his, decorated by some professional idiot, should belong to a Colombian drug lord.

He stops at the double doors and raises his eyebrows at me. I put my hands in his hair to muss it, to shake out the public and make a private mess for myself.

'Did you see Billy's face when Tom won? He's such a bad actor, he couldn't even hide it for one close-up. I hope the camera caught it.'

'Your look was good.'

'Yeah?'

'Do it now,' I tell him. He likes me to give him commands, sometimes.

He makes the losing face, giving it a hint of the best man won, and I laugh.

'You're too good,' I tell him. 'I'll go shoot the others and get that award for you.'

'I'm so glad I employ you,' he says. He fiddles with the top button of his shirt. 'These are so small. Jesus, help, I'm trapped in this thing.'

But talk of the job has cut through the come-ons. 'I've got to do a sweep first.'

'And bring the meds.'

'Bloody Americans, with your meds. Pills, love, we've got to take the pills.'

'So do it.'

'I am!'

'So go.'

To show him that I can, I walk away, but he knows he owns me. He has since Paris, the city of love, where the skin traders lurk on every corner from the dingy market stalls on the banks of the Seine to the Galleries Lafayette. Love comes in all price ranges.

No, not Paris in my thoughts now – I need a clear head. I bring out my baton from the inside pocket of my jacket. It puts my brain in the right place to make my sweep. From room to room, quick and quiet. I go outside for a word with the perimeter guard. Mike's on tonight, monitoring the screens from the booth by the main gate. He's good; he's a safe pair of hands. After our conversation I stand on the gravel driveway and look west, out over the Downs, and all the land Max owns. These are protected grounds where a deer herd is managed, and three full-time rangers ride their quad bikes like it's a racing track. I raised it with Max once and he said, 'I'm getting an easy ride, so why shouldn't they?'

I get it. I really do. But the people that feed on him make me angry. I make myself angry, sometimes, for being yet another parasite. But not tonight. The stars are out and the cold slice of the air upon my lips makes me want him more.

So I go back into the house and fetch the pills in the bathroom that's the size of my aunt's bungalow in Bristol. The pills are orange and tiny; they're another reminder of Paris. The guy who sold them to us looked over his shoulder the entire time. He didn't open the envelope to check the money Max gave him. He just pocketed it and scuttled back into the shadows of the Sacre Coeur. I suppose he thought he knew where he could find Max if he'd been ripped off. The whole world thinks it knows where it can find Max.

Only I know where to find Max right now. Through the cream double doors, and he is laid out on the four-poster bed with black silk sheets. Ridiculous, and mouthwatering.

I hand him a pill, and we swallow them down together.

The bodies, bodies together, are not love. Sex is not love, and I am not stupid. But we were in love before there was sex between us and surely that means something. It had built to something real before there was even that first tentative kiss. The body is just the instrument of the emotion; how can it be only in those cells and nowhere else? I'm overcomplicating this so I take off my clothes and leave the baton on the bedside table. I fold each article carefully before placing it on the ornate chair that must be worth more than a hundred skins.

'Any time,' Max says.

'You'll keep.'

'I'm too tired tonight.'

'Yeah yeah.'

He fakes a snore. His eyes are closed. We know this game. I tiptoe, and pounce. He's ready for me, he wraps me up, he says, 'I love you,' on an exhalation, like the words escape from inside him. 'Let me,' he says, and we roll so I'm lying on my front and he can stroke my back. He likes to touch more than to be touched. He makes love, breathes his love upon me. I feel it. As the moments pass, I feel it in every place where he puts his fingers and his mouth.

'Tell me about your first kiss,' he says.

I shake my head against the pillow.

'Just give me something. Some piece of you.'

He begs me on the bad nights, but I won't ruin this with the past. 'I do give you everything. Everything that's right here and now is yours.'

'I feel like I don't know you.'

'You know me,' I tell him. 'You're in me.'

Afterwards, he sleeps, and my skin starts to itch.

My skin is loosening.

It's starting to fall away.

I get up.

This can't be happening, it wasn't meant to happen, the pills – a last hope – to the bathroom, for more pills, and I take one, then two, then all of them in mechanical movements. I don't know if I'm trying to stop the process or stop myself from moving on.

I lie down on the tiles, so warm from the underfloor heating. It's easy to be still. The sensation of itchiness builds as my top layer of skin separates, starting around my stomach until it is a loose flap in which fluid moves, like a blister. It's so quick this time. The need to scratch cannot be ignored any more. The pills do nothing, I have to face that now; they neither kill me nor save me. What a waste of money. What a waste.

I rub myself against the tiles in a frenzy of itching until the skin splits, spilling forth fluid, and I can wriggle free of it. Then I know no more until morning.

> • <

I wake to find Max standing over me.

'The meds didn't work,' he says.

He holds out a hand that I don't take. I lie still. From the corner of my eye I can see my old skin, beside me, light and delicate as a shroud. I touch it, and for a moment I feel last night, and all the nights back to Paris and before.

I stop touching it. I look up at Max, naked Max, the film star; so many people would pay for this view. I wish he was wearing some clothes. I wish we both were.

'We should get dressed,' I say, and that is enough to give it all away.

'Oh shit, Rosie,' he says. He crouches down beside me and strokes my face while I wonder how long I have to let him.

2003. **IN TRAINING.**

Rose, alone, ran after the bobbing ponytail and implacable back of the instructor in the distance. Her breathing wouldn't fall naturally with the timing of her feet and the pain built quickly in her lungs and calves. Perhaps it was the uneven ground that made it so much harder than it should have been. Squashing the reedy grass underfoot, tramping down nettles, she kept going, wishing she'd worn long jogging trousers rather than shorts.

When the instructor – Petra – came to a sudden halt, Rose's pride stopped her from dropping to the ground. She bent over, put her hands on her knees. Her legs were freely decorated with white welts and fine red scratches. She sucked in air, over and over. The day was cold but she didn't feel it, only the awareness of it, the wind careering around her, unable to touch the warmth inside.

'I thought you said you kept yourself pretty fit?' said the instructor, through measured breaths.

Rose straightened up. 'It's the ground.' Back in the direction they had come, the disused airbase was no longer visible.

'City running.'

'It'll get better.'

Petra slid a hand along the dark length of her ponytail, pulling the weight of it over one shoulder. 'You don't need to do that. Make excuses. I'm not your boss.'

'Okay,' said Rose.

'This isn't my job, I mean. I just help Phin out sometimes, and he helps me out. In return.'

'How?'

'What?'

'How does he help you out?'

Petra shook her head. The ponytail bounced. She looked like the perfect image of a personal trainer: so upright, so together. 'You're ex-RAF, right? Then a bouncer.'

'Yeah.'

'And now about to become a bodyguard.' She opened and closed her fingers in bursts. 'To Max Black, no less. It's a good gig.'

'Right.' Rose looked along the line of the hedgerow, into the indiscernible distance. It wasn't a city. That was all it needed to be, right now.

'I hope you like bodyguarding. I did.'

'You guarded Mr Black?'

'No. Some other rich good-looking dream. Then I woke up.'

A closer look at Petra's face showed a hint of age, but she was by no means an old woman. Still, she wore that soft expression when talking of the past.

'You miss it,' Rose said.

'We all move on.'

That, at least, was certain. We all move on. Whether we want to or not.

'Let's get back for lunch,' said Petra, and was gone, running at a steady, speedy pace. Rose squared her shoulders, sucked in a breath, and set off after her.

Later, at Petra's house, Rose took a hot shower and the sensation was of her lassitude being washed from her, puddling around her feet and circling the plughole. She was fully awake for what felt like the first time since leaving the RAF. If she ran again now, she would do better.

The steam rushed and tumbled from the window as soon as she released the catch, and the cold poured in to take its place. She looked out over the airbase: the empty hangars and the silent stretch of the runway, the encroaching weeds spotting it all with green. So still, and so different from what she was used to. To be without people was good, though. To be separate, and to have space.

Apart from Petra, who was waiting downstairs in the kitchen with a chicken salad sandwich, the bread cheap and white, the tomatoes overripe and tasty.

'How long were you a bodyguard?' Rose asked, in between bites.

'Four years. Then I went into business on my own.'

'Doing what?'

'You wouldn't believe me if I told you.' She had changed into a fresh tracksuit, black and businesslike. 'Being a bodyguard opens doors to all sorts of worlds. That's the main thing. You meet people. Just don't fall for any bullshit.'

'Phineas said the clients were all in the entertainment business.'

'That's what I mean. It's all glamour and promises. And you're never on the inside. Nobody is, really.'

They ate standing up, with plates on the work surface next to the sink. Petra switched on the kettle, and the soft, building noise filled the room.

'It's so quiet here,' Rose said.

'It's my hideaway. The MOD sold these houses off for next to nothing when they closed down the base. Old military quarters. Plus nobody's watching the place any more so it's a perfect location for training. It's not guarded; I cut a hole in the fence and I come and go as I want. Weapon practice.

That stuff. Miles of unused ground. Of course, you'll know most of it already. That's why you only get the week-long refresher.'

Rose finished the sandwich. She could have eaten another but didn't know if she should ask. To what extent was this, the whole thing, a test?

'If you could tell me one thing that I should know, what would it be?'

Petra chewed her mouthful, taking her time, and swallowed. 'At some point, it will end. Tea?'

'Yes please. Everything does, though.'

'Not like this does. Leaving you sorry you ever got close to it. Almost believing the lie that life is so much better for some lucky, beautiful, chosen people. And then you end up somewhere else, and it all seems like it never happened. So remember who you are, down inside. The thing that is most you.'

'Right,' said Rose.

'You know what I mean?'

'Yep.'

'No you don't,' Petra said, as she took down two mismatched mugs from a cupboard.

'No,' Rose agreed. 'I don't.'

2013. **STOLEN SKIN.**

There are sad cases and happy ever after stories everywhere, and sometimes there are both rolled up in the same skin.

I told Terence, once, about the Grecian vase, the neon fish tank and the awards ceremonies. That life reflected in his eyes, a sparkling dream, and he said, 'You had it all, then, Rose.' Then the glitter faded. The smell of second-hand clothes kicked into his nostrils once more, and his mind couldn't put the two together. I saw it so clearly, the moment when he decided I was pulling his leg.

'Good one,' he said. 'Good one.' He went back to sorting out the contents of the bin bags.

The Skin Disease Centre makes a good amount in charitable donations from this little shop. It's set up in the far corner of the reception area, behind the rows of plastic chairs, and we squeeze as much as we can on to the racks and shelves: clothes, books, trinkets and teacups. The back room is piled even higher with items waiting to be given the chance to sell; my hand gets tired with pricing it all with the ancient sticker gun. Ten pence for this coaster, a pound for that cardigan.

But hey, it's just a tired hand attached to a tired body. It's not fatal. When you fall a long way for a long time and a cushion provides a soft landing, you don't complain that it smells bad and has had six previous owners. That last job should have been the end of me, but here I am.

That's why it's not right that he should come walking in, eight years after I shed him, looking like he's too good for the place. Which he is.

'Max Black,' I say. 'Superstar.'

'Still just Max to you.' He smiles.

'Not to the rest of the world.' He walks on water, and everything turns to liquid around him for his ease. It ripples to his touch. So many words, so much adoration, for the actor turned director. I read on a gossip website that he was making a film about the Stuck Six. 'Were you just passing?'

He browses, actually browses, a circular rail of men's shirts. 'Something like that.'

'Sussex and Lincolnshire must have got closer together since the last time I checked. You are still in Sussex?'

He hesitates, then nods. He picks a tartan shirt from the rail, with frayed cuffs and collar, and fingers the sleeve.

'That crazy house,' I muse.

'I timed this for lunch,' he says. 'Let me take you to lunch.'

'Why?'

'Because you loved me once.'

That was the last thing I expected him to say. I'm aware of Terence's attention, ears pricking up, in the back room. I get this vision of him leaning forward over a bin bag of clothes, straining to catch every word. He's so young, only one skin out of school.

'Terence,' I call. 'Can you watch the shop for an hour?'

No reply.

I pull open the curtain and find him just as I imagined, except the bin bag contains romance novels, the covers dog-eared and shiny.

'Terence.'

'Yeah?'

'Hold the fort.'

'Yeah,' he says. But he's not looking at me. He's looking behind me, at Max Black, and his sparkling eyes are saying - it was true. It was all true.

> • <

'He's in love with you,' says Max.

'Who?'

'The kid. In the thrift store. Terence.'

'Don't be stupid.'

Max shrugs. He's comfortable here, sure of his own thoughts in the back of his bulletproof Range Rover. There was no point in attempting a cafe, a restaurant, anything normal. His bodyguard would have to clear the place first and the staff wouldn't leave him alone. Thus speaks the voice of experience. But here, parked up near the bus station, we can talk and his bodyguard – a good-looking woman, of course – can wait outside in the car park for however long it takes. She won't like it, but she'll do it.

'I thought you were a private investigator or something,' he says. 'Last time we spoke you were working in London. Instead you do a disappearing act and I have to hire someone to track you down. What happened?'

'I shed.'

'You're so weird,' he says, in an angry rush, as if the words had to escape out of him, 'You are so fucking weird, Rosie. You could have just called me if you needed money. We were – we were so happy. If you were in trouble, you could have called.'

'If I ever am in trouble, I'll bear that in mind.' I open a cubbyhole in the central console and find a half-bottle of champagne, unopened, and a glass. Underneath that there's a packet of mints.

'You may find this ironic,' he says, 'but it turns out I'm the one in trouble.'

I can't even begin to get my head around that one. 'What kind of trouble?'

'I got robbed.'

'Get real.' He's never alone, he's never vulnerable. He hires people to make sure of it.

'The Sussex house got turned over. A professional job.'

'What did they take?' I know the answer before he says it.

'The skins.'

'They got into the safe room?'

I saw that room being built. I liaised about the safety features. It was Fort Knox in the South Downs. It was unbreakable.

It was asking for trouble. I find I'm not surprised. But the skins – that's a different matter. The skins are a big deal. The thought of someone else having them makes my insides hurt. I'm suddenly grateful this isn't my problem; Max burned my old skin. I watched him light the bonfire. The only skins in that room were his own.

If he was a normal person he would have burned his own, long ago, or sold them for a few pounds. But the rich and famous, they don't do normal things. They keep every single shedded skin, and it's the fashion to have special temperature-controlled rooms for them. There are so many people out there who want a tiny piece of a celebrity to call their own.

'Check the top-end businesses,' I say. 'They'll try to shift them on the quiet.'

Max shakes his head. 'We checked. They're not moving through the usual channels. Whoever took them is keeping them, for now.' He wets his lips, then says, 'Find them for me.'

'I don't do that any more. That wasn't what I did, anyway, exactly. I wouldn't be any good at this.'

'You knew people, right? Someone in the trade took my skins. I don't want anybody else to have them. I know you understand this.'

It's difficult to think clearly about skins from the past. I don't want to be near those old loves, to touch them, or feel them. But, like Max, I don't want anyone else to, either. Particularly the skin in which Max once loved me.

'I don't understand you,' he says. He takes a card from the pocket of his shirt and holds it out. 'My private number, if you change your mind. I can pay well. But then, it's not about the money, is it? Or the love. If you work out what the hell it is about, let me know.' He signals and the bodyguard opens the door, so I climb out and stand in the car park, watching him drive away until I can't see the car any more.

I can't quite believe he left me here. It's a fair walk back to the shop.

I look at the card.

MAX

it says, and then a number. He doesn't even need a surname any more.

A bus will take me back in the right direction.

While I ride, I take out my phone and browse online. I start off with looking for stories about him. Is he in a relationship? Well, I'd never find the truth by searching through the gossip sites. But the pictures show him with people, of course. All kinds of people.

The skyscraper ads are all about love.

It makes our world go round; the merry spin of who is in love, out of love. A story catches my eye about the Stucks. Six of them, in love with each other at the same time, once upon a time, but now the magic is over and their story is about to be turned into a thing of cinematic beauty, courtesy of Max Black. The photo of them at the top of the article shows them in the midst of that miracle of timing, all holding hands and smiling with rare radiance.

If only other emotions were lost in the moult. Fear, pain, guilt, sadness: why must these remain? Some people say it's because those emotions are true, lasting, while love could never survive for longer. But I think love is the strongest feeling of all, and that's why it has to die, and be sloughed away. Otherwise it could kill us. I remember how I would have taken a bullet for Max, or murdered someone who threatened him. Surely I'm better off without those feelings.

I'm better off being the kind of person who won't even make a few enquiries for him.

Fear, pain, guilt. Sadness.

When I reach the Skin Centre I stand outside the doors and call the number on the card. To his credit, he answers the phone himself and has the decency to sound surprised.

'Okay,' I tell him. 'I'll poke around. But that's all. I have a life here.'

'I know,' he says. 'I saw it.'

'What does that mean?'

'It means thank you. I know how hard this must be for you. I didn't realise—'

I cut him off, and go back to work.

2005. **LEAVING THE ONCE LOVED.**

Petra's office, once Rose finally located it, turned out to be in one of those back alleys that had been squeezed into the shadows of other buildings. A supermarket depot jostled up behind it, the two separated only by a high wall upon which had been arranged a regiment of broken bottles. Hammersmith Road was in front, the cars bunching up and loosening in a continuous concertina.

It was locked up tight. She pressed the doorbell, and an outline appeared through a small central panel of leaded glass.

'It's Rose,' she said.

The unbolting of the door took an age.

'I could have lost another layer, that took so long,' she said, when Petra's face was finally revealed. She felt the muscles of her cheeks contorting but refused to cry. Petra wasn't the kind of person she felt she could cry on.

Petra pointed at her leather backpack. 'Is that all?'

'What?'

'You shed your skin on the floor of a superstar, then break up your fabulous romance, and that's all you bring? I expected at least one suitcase filled with money, or statuettes, or something.'

'I don't want to take anything of his.'

'Don't be such an idiot.'

'I can't help it. Can I come in?'

'Yes, sorry, manners. Come up, come up.' She stood back and admitted Rose to the tiny hall that led to a steep wooden staircase. 'Space is money. The door on the left.'

The bolts were slammed back into place behind her, and

then she heard Petra's fast feet drumming up the stairs. The room on the left was a surprise: larger than she thought it would be, and lighter, with tall windows. It had a half-moon shaped pine desk in one corner, and a rubber plant in a bronze pot opposite. The plant exuded health, the shiny leaves tilted upwards. Apart from that, there was a yellow chaise longue with scrolled arms, squarely in the centre of the room, and an open fireplace with a pillared mantelpiece, painted white. Upon it were stacked letters and bills, photos and manila folders, and a silver lighter. But the room did not smell of smoke, and there was no ashtray in sight.

'You told Phin?'

'Yeah,' said Rose. 'Now what?'

'Now you come and work for me. With me, if you prefer. Is that okay?'

She nodded.

'I'm an investigator. Fancy being one of those?'

Could this new skin be an investigator's skin? She wondered at how quickly she had left her last self behind. The self-assurance of the bodyguard, wiped away. But she already knew, this time around, that what she had lost in confidence she had gained in curiosity. There was so much she wanted to know, such as why the love disappeared and how the hate managed to stay behind, intact. If there were answers to be found to any question, she wanted to do it. 'What do you investigate?'

'The worst things.'

'Do you stop them?'

'Always,' Petra told her. There wasn't a speck of doubt to be found on her in that sharp suit. She inhabited the office, and the work. Whatever it was. 'Always. One way or another.'

2013. UNGUARDED.

A leave of absence from the shop is the hardest part to arrange. Head Office wants a return date. Eventually we settle on a Monday a month away, and I don't mark it on the calendar, which tells me something about my state of mind.

It's not even as if my moult is due. I should have at least another five years, but I feel done with this version of my life already.

The fast train from Grantham, then from King's Cross to Waterloo, an easy journey out of rush hour. I try to ignore the tight feeling London gives me in my chest; is it simply the stale air of the Underground? Down to Petersfield, which is a tight, monied kind of a town, secure in itself. I decide once I get there to hire a car rather than take a taxi using the expenses card Max had couriered up for me. The note that came with it bore his handwriting, but didn't tell me anything useful such as how much of his money I could spend, or how much he would be paying me. I'm guessing he didn't even think about such issues.

The approach to his Sussex house is the same: undeveloped stretches of rural land for so many miles around, green fields, dotted trees that darken the sky. But then, he owns it all, so the current building boom wouldn't affect him. The tall fence with the high spikes still runs alongside the road for miles, and then broadens out into a set of gates – chunky, not flashy. Definite in their discouragement. I pull up to the metal pillar that houses the intercom and have a short conversation with a guy who sounds familiar, but I'm not certain that it's Mike until I'm admitted and he comes out of the booth beside the beginning of the gravel drive to greet me. I get out of the car and find myself giving him a genuine smile.

'Look at you,' Mike says, holding out his arms and then dropping them again before I can mistake it for the offer of a hug. 'You look great.'

'You look the same,' I tell him. He really does. 'Don't you age? I can't believe it, eight years and here you are.'

'Ah, well, it's just a job. I never get the itch after a moult the way some people do.' Then he flushes, and I realise he's embarrassed.

'I have to get out straight after. Same every time. Sorry I never said goodbye. It's just how it takes me.'

He nods and we're over the awkward moment. 'Mr Black said you were coming to see the safe room. They cracked it without a scratch. I've never seen anything like it.'

'Were you on duty?'

'Yep, and nobody came through here. I've checked the perimeter since, twice. It's intact.'

'Nobody through the gate – not even a legit caller? A girlfriend, boyfriend?'

'Nobody. The only thing that was different that day was Taylor – the bodyguard – changed her day off. The replacement came down, signed in early in the morning, and stayed until the following morning. She's covered for Taylor before, she's all right. But she said she didn't hear anything. Max took two sleeping pills and was out like a light. He's lucky they didn't strip him of the skin he's in now.'

It's a horrible crime, but I've heard of worse. 'Max in?'

'Filming on the estate. He's got a village set up there, caravans and everything, for this new thing he's working on. Nobody's staying at the house.'

'So there's a lot of people out on the Downs, then? Actors and crew?'

'Fifty plus.'

I roll my eyes and he smiles. It's a security nightmare, basically. 'I'll have to go poke around.'

'Starting in the house, though, right?'

'Yep.'

'It's great to have you around,' he says. He leans forward. 'None of the ones who have come after have been a patch on you.' He gives me a set of codes and leaves me to it. I was unprepared for the emotion, but it really is good to see him.

In contrast, the house is not a welcome sight. It gives me that uncomfortable sensation straight away – like I'm done with it, and should have left it behind. At least the decor is different. Out with the neon, the vases, and in with dark wood and rich red tapestries, even a vast open fireplace. This latest designer obviously believes in the classic English Lord look, and has succeeded in making the place too warm, too close, for my liking.

I walk the corridors and find myself in the bathroom where I lost my love for Max. It's different too; tiled purple, with more dark wood around the edges, almost black. A framed pen-and-ink drawing of the Eiffel Tower, just a few lines creating the feeling of the city, hangs over the clawfoot bathtub.

I could be sick.

I hunch over the toilet.

The feeling passes, and I straighten up and check in the bathroom cabinet. Max always was a believer in pills, all kind of pills, but I don't see any, not even the sleeping aids Mike was talking about. Perhaps the last couple of moults have changed that aspect of his personality; who knows what's been taken, and what he's willingly thrown away? Besides, that's not my business. My business is the safe room, in the basement. So that's where I go, and the shock of seeing that thick metal door left open, and the temperature-controlled wardrobe emptied, bare, is considerable. It's a forlorn, forgone expensive space with those skins missing. A collected life history has been taken.

Besides that, there are some building materials down here; he must be having some work done to the place. Strengthened, perhaps, for the return of his skins? Max always did believe in the best possible outcome.

We've not discussed it, but I'm fairly certain the police haven't been here. There are no signs of an investigation. Max wouldn't want them poking around.

Besides, there's nothing to see. No points of interest. Nothing was forced, nothing was damaged. Whoever did this had the door code. Which means I need to talk to the bodyguards – the one who was on duty, and the one who had the incredible foresight to not be.

She seems efficient. I'd guess he isn't sleeping with her, the way she talks about him, but I was good at maintaining that distance in public, back when protecting him was my job. To stand behind someone, at the ready, without touching, looking at them only with the professional gaze in place, is an easy trick to learn. You use it no matter what your feelings about your client, or you endanger them. Some of Petra's lessons have lasted.

'You ex-Forces?' I ask her.

'Navy.'

'Then you got hooked up with Starguard?'

'Phin approached me in a bar. I was bouncing there.' She smiles. So Phineas Spice has been up to his same old tricks. She looks fond of him; it's easy to like him, even though it's not sensible to.

'Been here long?'

'About a year.'

She checks behind me – over my shoulder – that Max is still in her line of vision. We're sitting in canvas chairs next to the catering wagon, which is offering a range of breakfast goodies that I struggled to resist. My croissant looks good on the plate but soon disintegrates into a mess of crumbs. At least the Americano is hot and fresh. Back when I was on the job I never would have eaten, and I'm pleased to see Taylor feels the same. She's sipping a mint tea.

'You like the work?' I ask her.

'It's better than bouncing, am I right?' So she's recognised me as ex-Forces too, with all the bad choices that come along after that stint – or perhaps Phin told her about me. That wouldn't surprise me at all.

She frowns at something behind me, so I turn and look at Max, who is talking to a tall man with curly black hair – it might even be one of the Stucks, he looks familiar – and pointing at the sun, which is about to disappear behind a scudding cloud. Everyone is milling about, looking grumpy. Film work always did look more like standing around than doing.

'It's okay,' Taylor says, 'just outdoor filming stuff. He's about to lose the sun. He'll probably break for ten minutes.

Well, you probably know that.'

'I've never seen him as a director before. It looks like he enjoys it.'

'Jobs,' she says. 'They come and go.'

Her reflective tone annoys me; I'm not here to talk philosophy. 'The night of the skin robbery – you weren't here.'

'No. It was my night off. You know the drill.'

I do know the drill, well. One night off a fortnight, arranged in advance. 'But you changed yours at short notice.'

'Family emergency,' she says, shortly.

I don't see any point in pushing her. 'So you did a handover with your replacement?'

'Yeah. I only know her as Smith.'

'Seriously?'

She glares at me. 'Obviously that's not her real name. She's legit, though. Tall. From Korea, Phin said. She was a skin fighter, and he bought her contract.'

'Smith the Korean skin fighter.' Only in film star circles. If she really was in the skin fights then she's hard as nails, but it crosses my mind that it might be a story to make her seem glamorous to the kind of people who get off on that stuff. My bodyguard used to be a hooker, that kind of line. People in the entertainment business can be downright weird.

'Ten minutes,' calls Max. 'Ten minutes, everyone.'

Taylor finishes her tea and stands. I get up too, and wonder if I once looked that good. She has that fearless, appraising gaze; the one I tried to find early this morning when I put on a dark grey suit for the first time in years. I stood in front of the wardrobe and willed myself back to that alert stance, but it just wouldn't come.

'I have to go. Listen, you should be asking Smith this stuff. It was her shift, so it's her mistake.'

Now I know I don't like Taylor. She's happy to drop Smith in it quick enough.

'A mistake?' I give her room to elaborate, but she swallows, and then only offers a nod. 'We all make mistakes, though, don't we?' I can't resist saying, just to see how much she rattles, and a familiar voice behind me says, 'Don't bother trying to win an argument with her, Taylor. It can't be done.'

I spin, and smile, and shake Max's proffered hand, even though the contact must be unpleasant for both of us. The feeling of wrongness that comes from revisiting the past isn't anywhere near as strong for other people; I must remember that. Perhaps he barely feels this need to put distance between us. Some people, like my parents, even manage to stay civil after moulting. It's a trick I'll never master, with my condition.

'You're paying me to ask the difficult questions,' I say.

'Nope. I'm paying you to get the difficult answers. I'll start you off. Taylor didn't have a personal reason for changing her night off. She was running an errand for me. One that's best kept quiet.'

'Pills?'

He inclines his head. It's always pills, with him. The endless pills that never work. To his credit, he doesn't bother to explain it.

'I'll need the name of your supplier.'

'Really?'

'They knew Taylor would be out collecting your order. Possibly they've got something on Smith, or suspected she wouldn't be up to the task. It was a good opportunity to take what they really wanted.'

'No, it's not that kind of an organisation, I swear, Rosie.'

'Max, I have to check.'

He breathes out, his chest deflating, then asks Taylor for a pen and piece of paper, which she produces from her suit pocket. He writes down a name and address, and hands it to me.

'Chichester? Not exactly a den of iniquity.'

'I told you – they're not the usual kind of people.' He checks his watch, and strides off. No goodbye. Taylor throws me a glance, and then goes with him.

As I slip the address into my pocket I feel my phone vibrate. It's a message from another person I thought I'd left in my past, and it means Chichester has to wait.

I need to get to London, fast.

> • <

It's a difficult business, identifying old skins. The feeling you get from touching one is only a reflection of the love the old owner once felt, before it was sloughed away. If it was a particularly strong love you might get images accompanying the feeling: a flash of a face, or maybe even a snatch of music. Still, it's like piecing together a puzzle, reconstructing an old photograph that's been torn to pieces.

Love is a Warm Layer

says the poster on the dingy green wall. There's a Labrador puppy wrapped in a blue blanket underneath the words. His face peeks out from the folds of material. I shift my position in the moulded plastic seat. My armpits are sweaty; I'll have to keep my arms by my sides if I don't want anyone to smell me. Which I don't. This kind of place reminds me how much I want my smell to be my own business.

The door opens, and in comes a small man, wearing a cream suit with a buttoned waistcoat. His shoes are imitation animal skin. I remember how I used to rely on my instant judgements, back when I was trying to learn this stuff as an occupation, and I would have said with no hesitation that this man was a petty criminal, dressing in the hope of getting better at it. Do I trust my judgements any more? I keep my face blank, non-committal, as I stand. The receptionist, an older woman who keeps knitting on the desk next to the phone, eyes us both with interest.

'Rose Allington?' he says. It's an Eastern European accent. 'Petra said to wait for you. She said you would come today, but I have other buyers. There's a line for this one, I can move it—' He snaps his fingers at me.

'I'm here. I want it, if it is what you say it is.'

'It is. But you don't need to take my word for it.'

'Of course. Where is it?'

'This way.'

The receptionist's head has been snapping back and forth during our exchange like a spectator at a tennis match.

'Margot,' he says, 'hold calls.'

'Of course.' She turns to me and winks. It's unbelievable. She thinks she's in a stage play, or something – that her life as a gangster's receptionist is not real. Maybe she moulted and woke up with the urge to leave her comfortable life behind, and this is the result; enjoying the seedy workings of a company that the world would be better off without.

I follow him through the door and down a long corridor with peeling paint and exposed pipes, my mind taken up with that wink. Is that how it gets, after one too many moults? Everything becomes an in-joke?

His office is at the end; it's a small room, with a painting placed to draw the eye above a single high-backed velvet armchair, the seat worn shiny. The painting is meant to look very old but something tells me it's not. It's a reproduction of a suffering saint who wears a white robe, diaphanous, that shimmers around him – no, it's his skin coming free. He's in the death throes of the final moulting. His eyes are raised to heaven, and radiance comes from him as he sloughs off his last skin, and leaves this mortal life.

An alcove is curtained off; the man, name still unknown to me and I'd like to keep it that way, pulls back the thick purple material. There, folded neatly upon a long trolley, is a skin. It looks as light and ordered as a sheaf of papers.

'Full out,' I say. I know the tricks.

'You don't want to touch first?'

'Full out.'

He lifts it and arranges it, to make it into the shape of a body once more, and I know instantly that it's not one of Max's.

'You're wasting my time.'

'Wait.'

'It's not even male.' The breasts have been cut away and the remaining material sewn together to create a flatter chest that would fool nobody in the skin trade. I could leave. I should leave.

'Just touch it,' says the nameless man.

I put my fingers to the long, flat tube of the nearest arm and let the emotion come to me.

Yes, that's love, the remains of it, the whisper that dies away from the shout and can never quite be silenced. Love for Max, specifically, undeniably; I'm getting it clearly now, the feeling as precise as a signature. Not fan adoration, not a crush, which is different. This is the real deal. Deep, and reciprocated. Requited love, soaked into the skin.

I see Max for a moment as I once saw him. He's the bridge of the song, the voice of happy ever after. He's how to live, and why.

The feeling fades.

He was my reason to write bad poetry; thank God I never was one for recording my emotions. I can't quite believe how I felt about him, just as I can't believe that anybody else ever did.

This is my skin.

My skin, here, in this crumbling back office, the breasts mutilated in the name of money. Max told me he'd burned it. I watched him walk it out to the bonfire.

I pull back my hand.

'See? Not fake.'

I can tell from his expression that he doesn't know it once belonged to me.

'I'll take it,' I say. 'What's your price?'

He touches his tongue to his top lip and names a huge sum. Max's very first moult itself wouldn't cost more. We haggle, and I knock him down a little, but nowhere near as much as I should. I have no taste for this. I need that skin, and that's all there is to it.

But I also need one more thing, and I have to time it

right, so I wait until the deal is struck and the skin has been refolded and wrapped in brown paper, and the money is about to be transferred from Max's credit line, before I say, 'I'll need the details.'

'What?'

'Provenance. Who sold it to you?'

'That's not— I don't—'

'Details.' I plant my feet squarely, make it clear I won't move without it. 'It's necessary. Or we can cancel.'

He's already pictured the money in his account; he's not going to lose it now. 'It was a charity shipment. Random bag. I have people who go through, checking for pure ones. We got lucky.'

'You did,' I agree, although I know nobody gets that lucky. But it's not his bluff. My instincts, long unused and struggling to surface, tell me that he really believes in this random bag story. Which means he's part of the setup.

'We're done,' I tell him, and I complete the transaction on my phone. He leads me out, a different path this time, down a flight of stairs and through a warehouse with thin, dirty windows where women and machines are hard at work. Skins are being sorted, pressed, scissored and stitched to make skimpy underwear. Love is a warm layer, indeed.

Back out on the street I find a familiar franchise of cafe and call Petra, who asks me if her tip was good. She doesn't question me when I ask her instead where it came from. She was once my partner; she knows who to trust, and when. We worked together every day before this last moult of mine, and we were good at it.

'Don't drop me in it, Rose,' she says.

'It never came from you.'

So she gives me a name – a name that I've already heard today.

I finish my call and eat a slice of cake, savouring the sweetness. I have gone soft; I'm running on caffeine and sugar. A text message comes in.

Max: *Either u found them or that's a big dinner allowance you just gave yourself.*

Rosie: *Not one of your skins. A necessary purchase. Will explain later.*

Max: *Looking 4ward to it. Where are u?*

How strange it is, to see our names next to each other on the screen.

I don't reply. I open my leather backpack and look at the brown paper package inside. To buy it cost more money than I'll ever make in my life. Luckily, it's not my money. And I had to have it; Max will understand that. Particularly because this is his fault. If he had burned it as I asked, as he told me he had, it wouldn't have been sitting in his skin room when the thieves took the lot.

So now I have to carry my old skin with me until I can find the time to dispose of it properly. I don't want to be close to it, but there's no choice. It's now become part of this puzzle.

And the man who holds the next piece is Phineas Spice.

2006. LIGHTER.

London wasn't so much a place as a mismatched mosaic of a city. The buildings looked sturdy enough, but the colours weren't coherent. One backdrop was bright, the next clouded, and the pieces of people were dotted so randomly, an arm here, a head there. Rose never felt that she saw a whole person, only glimpses of expressions in a sharp-edged cut-out compilation.

She saw it differently to Petra, she knew. Petra found form and shape in everything because of the way it settled around her; she was her own centre. But Rose, sitting in her sleeping bag on the floor of the dark office, waiting for Petra's return, worried she would never learn how to be that way.

She leaned her head against the wall, and the manila folder slipped from her lap to the cream carpet, the documents and photographs splaying out like a fan. There they were – what Petra would have called the worst things.

The only way these kinds of pictures, this kind of knowledge, made sense was if a person said to herself – some people aren't right. They aren't right in the head.

Them and us.

Or Rose could say – I'd never do a thing like that, but how could she be sure? What lay under the next skin, and the next?

But no, easier to say she'd never pay to watch people rip each other's skin to shreds, and call it entertainment. The folder covered most of the details of skin fighting in the ring they had been investigating: the betting system, the location, the weapons specially designed to rip and scar. One of the fighters' managers would call time, eventually, afraid of what might happen next. Because if you damaged the skin enough, the next shed wouldn't be clean, or easy. The pain could send a person out of their mind, or kill them, and only a very specific crowd wanted to bet on that kind of thing, Petra had told her.

Pictures of scars, of skins in shreds, making London's mosaic pieces, lay scattered upon the plush cream carpet of the office.

No, it made no sense. Except to Petra, who had investigated it on Phineas's behest, and made a decision about what needed to be done next.

Call the police? Rose had said, almost hopefully. The police would give everything shape, for her.

See this bloke? said Petra, pointing to a shot of the crowd in cinema-style seating, close to the cage. He is the police.

It was like a line from a film. Too slick to be true. But maybe, sometimes, life could be like a film. For some people.

It was getting late. The concertina of traffic on the Hammersmith road was down to a soft squeeze. Rose leaned forward in her sleeping bag and gathered up the documents. She put them back in the file.

Everything was in its place except for the silver lighter that lived on the mantelpiece. Petra had taken it with her. It wasn't the first time this had happened, but it was the first time Rose had asked to go along. She had been given a look of bemusement in return. Did it mean she wasn't ready?

Enough questions.

She slid down the wall to lie flat on the carpet. Petra would take the chaise longue when she came back in; unspoken rules stated it was her sleeping spot. The weekends they spent back in Wiltshire, compartmentalising with a fair amount of success. Sometimes work spilled over into the conversations, but mainly they ate sandwiches and ran over the fields with the pace and purpose of escapees.

It was good.

One weekend, a few months ago, Petra had said, I'm due a moult, I think I've started, and sure enough there was a skin to be taken to the nearby council-run incinerator the next morning. Nothing changed, and there was no drama to it. Petra was the same.

It doesn't bother me much, she said. Worse if I've got a partner, obviously, and then there's breaking up and all that, but they've never turned nasty on me.

Of all the pieces that made no sense, that was the one that made Rose suspect that if there was a God, he had it in for her personally. But that was not a good, or a true, thought, she constantly reminded herself.

Sleep came from nowhere and left just as suddenly, to the sound of the downstairs door opening. The grainy light of early morning, followed by Petra's feet on the stairs, their quick rhythm: and then she was in the room, just visible, with the smell of smoke unspooling from her black clothes. She moved to the desk, then to the mantelpiece, searching through the piles of paper.

'You okay?' whispered Rose.

'Yeah. I can't find—' She spotted the manila folder, beside Rose. 'Is that it?'

'I was just looking through it.'

'What for?' Petra squatted and picked up the file. The smell of her was appealing in its thickness. It had its own presence in the room, speaking of an action completed.

After a pause, Rose said, 'I don't know.'

Petra patted her leg, through the sleeping bag. She took the file to the fireplace, and laid it in the grate. The silver lighter, produced from the pocket of her black leather coat, was flicked into life, and the file caught fire easily.

'Done,' said Petra. She stood, and stripped away her clothes. Her sports bra and pants were also black, sensible, and she looked lean. Fit for purpose, whatever that meant.

'How did it go?' whispered Rose. It was impossible to talk at a normal volume in the half-light.

'You know when you get rid of a skin you were really enjoying and its like watching the good stuff go up in flames? This is the opposite.'

'But won't they just set up another ring somewhere else?'

'Of course. It'll take them a few weeks, though.'

Petra wriggled into her sleeping bag, on the chaise longue. Rose listened to a long sigh escape her lungs.

'What good does it do, then?' she murmured.

'It helps me.'

'Helps you what?'

'Feel good about myself.'

'Is that all that matters?' said Rose, feeling a pain inside, a cutting emotion to which she couldn't begin to put a name. 'It's like… It's like you're the most important thing in your own universe.'

'I am. We all are. What I don't get is why you won't admit you should be the most important thing in yours.'

Later, when she was on the verge of finding sleep again, Petra said softly to her, 'Keep trying, Rose. One day you'll understand.'

2013. **AFTER STARGUARD.**

Is there really life after Starguard? Before this hunt kicked off I would have said yes. I had said my goodbyes to Phineas, and thought myself done with it all. Max bought me out, so there was no debt left to pay; I never expected to find myself willingly asking a favour of Phin again.

He sits at the polished glass bar of his club, sipping his vodka tonic. He's aged, but the eyes are the same. Untouched by the life, somehow immune to all complications of skin. He always did look a little greasy to the touch with that permanent tan; he shines under the club spotlights, as if it all slips away from him.

It's simple, he said to me, when Max paid him back for the clothes, the contacts, the cost of the opportunity. Don't ever fall in love. It's a choice.

He lived as if that were true. Perhaps it was, for him. A different partner every night, paid for so there was no chance to prefer one to the others. He never retraced his steps, that was the rumour.

If I make him sound like a monster then I've only explained one half of him, for all these things stem from the practicality that protects him. To live by your own rules and never deviate from them – that gives him a power that goes beyond charm. I do believe he has never meant to cause anybody deliberate harm. In fact, he's gone out of his way to shut down the worst excesses of human behaviour he's come across. But I now think it's all to protect the sweet soul that I sometimes glimpse in him, and if you get caught up in his defence mechanism then he'd only think you an idiot.

Still, I think he's always had a soft spot for me.

It's early evening for the club – before midnight – and it won't start heating up until after two. So right now the music is only soft jazz, and I don't have to raise my voice to make myself heard.

'I'm betting you already know why I'm here.'

'I knew you'd work it out, Rose. I hear you're up in Lincolnshire. How's that?'

'Different.'

'So why go back to the work now? Hanging clothes on racks not cutting it for you?'

'Max asked me,' I say. I take a sip of my mineral water.

'That's not it, though, is it? It was the thought of those old skins, being stroked. Being used. You would have moved on for good if he hadn't kept those old skins.'

'What do you do with yours?' I ask, giving in to the temptation to make it personal.

'Take them down the public incinerator,' he says. 'I know, that's not in fashion. I had you down for a burner too, but then this old skin popped up on the radar and I thought – nobody loved Max like you did. Then I heard about the burglary and it all made sense. Did he keep it without you knowing?'

'It was a misunderstanding.'

Phin raises an eyebrow. When I don't elaborate, he says, 'We wear ourselves, then we peel ourselves away. We change and we change. How strange it is, the things we become, and the things we throw away. Do you know that poem? One of the Stuck Six wrote it, after she moulted.'

'No.'

'Well. It's not important. I did you a favour, getting word to Petra before some crazy came along and snapped it up.'

'Thank you.'

'So let's say we're even. We've helped each other out enough for that, I think.'

He might mention things I'm desperate not to talk about. The warehouse flashes through my mind, so I move the conversation along. 'How did you hear about it?'

He smiles. 'It was being shouted out, Rose. Everyone was talking about it – the thefts, and then this appearance, from nowhere, of a prime Max Black contact skin, up close and personal, with the smell of sex on it.' I wince, and he pats my hand. 'Sorry, but that's how it was broadcast. There was nothing subtle about it. I'd watch your back, if you're carrying that skin around. There are lots of unscrupulous people in the game.'

I stand up. 'Thanks,' I say.

'You going to destroy it, then?'

'It should have been destroyed at the start.'

'Yes, it should,' he agrees.

I remember how much I like him. Like is different from love – it can survive. It's held in the brain, perhaps, and not the skin. Phin found me working clubs as a bouncer, considering moving into fighting or selling myself, and he set me up in a job. With Max. Then he let Max buy out my contract. It was all about money, but it was never cruel, and he could so easily have been cruel, considering all the things he's seen.

And then he was my employer again, in a different way. He still is Petra's employer. They both try to make themselves feel better about the world, and that's fair enough, I think. Yes, it's fair enough.

He once told me something about myself, that helped

me to make sense of the inexplicable. For that, along with everything else, I will forever think good thoughts of him.

I lean in and kiss his greasy cheek goodbye.

'I've got a gig minding Trad Prester,' he says. 'Two weeks, London, next month. Cash in hand, if you're interested, as a one-off. You still in shape?' He looks me up and down.

'Not even a little bit.'

'Ah well. You should do something about that before age catches up with you.'

'It already has.' I turn to leave, and then remember one more question I should ask. 'Smith. She was working for Max the night of the burglary. Can I speak to her? Is she here?'

'Smith?'

'Skin fighter you liberated. Korean.'

'Ahh…' He swallows, and the movement draws attention to the folds of skin around his Adam's apple, visible above the opening of his cream shirt. So he has aged, after all. 'No, you can't speak to her. She went back to fighting.'

'She chose to go back in?'

'Some of them do. They get the taste for it.'

'Where is she now?'

He shakes his head. 'Got in a nasty bout, nothing to do with me.'

'She's dead?'

'She was lovely,' Spice says. 'Straight off the container ship, they got her.'

'You got her out, though.'

He takes a long drink. 'Well, we didn't speak the same language anyway.'

'When was this?'

'Day before yesterday. It's all very fresh in the mind right now.' He taps the side of his head. 'Never mind. It'll pass.'

I don't ask him anything else. I leave it at that. Enough of London. I feel the same way about it as I feel about Phineas Spice. I have fond memories but I'll be damned if I make too many new ones.

> • <

A bad night's sleep in a cheap hotel later, I take the first train to Chichester. On the journey, the carriage window stuck half open and the businessman behind me shouting into his phone over the wind, I make a list of my skins:

Age 16 – first moult. Bristol. Gave it to Mum.

Age 21 – Early second moult triggered by stress. Finals at York tied with a break-up with Steve (who moulted me off). Burned the skin in a bin in the bedroom, the fire got out of control, fire brigade called, I got suspended. Joined the RAF.

Age 28 – Third moult while on active duty, Cyprus, established pattern of stressful moults. Kicked out of the RAF as unstable. Tried to bury the skin; the RAF took it and disposed of it properly as per regs.

Age 34 – Fourth moult. Sussex. Max told me he'd burned the skin.

Age 38 – Fifth moult. London. Sudden early moult, again triggered by stress. The warehouse. Skin was burned on the scrubland there.

My sixth moult is not due for another couple of years, at least, if things go according to the pattern.

So I have the fourth moult with me, in my backpack, and I will burn it as soon as the opportunity presents itself. That leaves only the first moult to account for. I know I'm only feeling paranoid, but I have to be sure that nobody can get to it. Even though the fourth skin, the one impregnated with Max, is the only one that could fetch big money. My first teenaged moult – well, there are people who would buy that for a few quid and a cheap rub from an online auction, but I'm not scared of those people. I only feel sorry for them.

But I need that skin gone anyway.

When Mum got ill my Aunt Alice took in her old skins. She'd been a hoarder all her life, and although I said they should be cremated along with her, Alice wouldn't hear of it. I hadn't thought about it before, but I suppose that means Alice still has my first skin too, so I need to find the time to return to Bristol.

But first I have to try to do my job.

2013. **ONE SKIN AWAY.**

The industrial estate on the south side of Chichester holds the usual small businesses for an affluent city: a curio shop next to a gym next to a vintage car mechanic next to a reclaimed antique tile seller. And in Unit 43B, tucked away at the dead end, there's the supplier of Max's damned pills. It's a clean white box of a building with blacked-out windows.

Mallory Peace Industries

It's better than the back streets of Paris, although I'm expecting to find the same kind of impossible promises inside. The pills we popped together once upon a time guaranteed current skin longevity. They were meant to give us longer in love. I wonder what Mallory Peace are selling him, and if he still wants to stay in the same skin forever. Perhaps, this time, he wants to speed up the process, or have the new skin underneath look younger. Does that sound like something Max would want? It's difficult to remind myself that I really don't know him any more.

There's a security camera over the main entrance, and a small intercom along the white wall. I push the little round button, not sure yet what I'm going to say. This is not how a proper private detective would do it. What would Petra lead with? Her voice won't come to me.

'Can I help you?' A man's voice: pretty young, I'd guess.

'Max Black sent me.' I don't elaborate.

I wait through the silence. The buzzer sounds, and the door swings back.

What's inside is a surprise.

Isn't that always the way, though? What's inside, behind, underneath that first layer, waiting to be found.

Focus, I tell myself.

The professional front is not a front at all. This really is a laboratory, an expensive operation, and the people I can see through the wall of safety glass that separates the workplace from the reception area are the real deal, with white coats and studious expressions. They are of all ages and colours, tapping on computers, using unidentifiable equipment; these aren't three college boys with bad hair, kitchen foil and a Bunsen burner.

Perhaps I should have expected better of Max.

No, no I shouldn't. He liked them on the seedy side. The back street exchanges, money in envelopes. He got a kick out of all that. This is a development; perhaps one that happened after a skin change.

The workers don't look at me. They must be used to visitors. This is certainly a room for that purpose alone – for the process to be observed. I look around me, at the upholstered chairs with curved arms and the pastel drawings of flowers on the walls. It reminds me of a dentist's waiting room.

I would sit quietly and wait but I tell myself that I'm here for a reason. I shouldn't have the patience or the personality type for waiting, right? Time is money. So I steel myself and tap on the glass. Everyone looks up, frowning in my direction. One of the white coats disengages from a computer and comes my way: an older woman with orange-rimmed glasses, bright, probably meant to be fun, but they give her a fierce and owlish look.

She puts her hands to the glass wall and a section slides

back. The waft of air from the laboratory is cool and sweet-smelling. 'Rose Allington?'

'Did Max tell you I'd be dropping in?'

'He did. He speaks highly of you. I'm Anna Mallory.'

We shake hands, and she slides the door closed behind her. So I'm not getting the guided tour.

'It's your name on the sign,' I say.

'One of them.'

'So Max deals with you directly?'

'He did, when he first signed up for the service. Since then he's not come in person. A young woman has picked up the treatment package. But we're expecting him in a month's time, for an evaluation. To see how it's going.'

The young woman – that would be Taylor, the bodyguard. 'What treatment package is he on?' I look around the room again, to make sure I haven't missed it. But no, there's no price list, no explanations. No written material at all.

'I'm afraid that's confidential,' she says.

'I have Mr Black's confidence.'

'In that case I suggest you ask him directly. How many questions do you have, Ms Allington? Should we sit down?'

'Yes,' I say. 'We should sit down.'

So we perch on the chairs, both bolt upright, and I ask far more questions than I had intended to, mainly to annoy her. To see if she can be annoyed. Which, apparently, she can't.

'Who knew about Mr Black's package? The times of delivery, say?'

'Me. Employees who deal with delivery preparation. They're all vetted carefully. I can supply you with a list of names, but I'd rather you didn't speak to them directly unless absolutely necessary.'

'How's your online security?'

'We employ a firm called Bastion Solutions to handle that. I took the liberty of asking them to check our records when Mr Black told me about the burglary. They reported no threats or compromises, but they are expecting your call.'

And so on, and so on. Every question I ask she's already thought of, and with every stonewall I find myself getting more and more curious as to what she's actually promised Max. Because she's the kind of person who doesn't promise what she can't deliver.

'When did you first meet Mr Black?' I ask her.

For the first time her eyes flicker. So here it is – a lie. 'Eighteen months ago.'

'Did you approach him, or did he come to you? How did he find out about you?'

'He phoned in an enquiry. I'd imagine he heard about us from somebody else in his line of work. We're quite well known in the entertainment industry now, and nearly all of our clients come through a personal recommendation.'

'Do you know which client recommended you to Max?'

She smiles. Well, of course she wouldn't answer that. But the smile is thin, and unamused. We're in territory she doesn't want to traverse.

'Okay,' I say. 'Never mind. I'll ask him myself. Can I get that list of names? Employees with access to Mr Black's records?'

'I'll email it. Could you?' She hands me a pen and a small orange notepad that matches the shade of her glasses. When I flip it open I find only pristine pages; it's brand new. I write my name, phone number and email address, feeling her eyes upon my writing.

'Thank you,' she says as I hand it back, and the way she says it makes me think that she's won this confrontation. Something important has passed between us and I don't even know what it is. Petra would have known. Petra would have solved this case by now.

We stand, and say polite goodbyes, before she taps in a code on the doorpad to release me back into the wild.

I walk to the hire car with no idea of what just really happened.

2007. BIG PICTURE.

It made for a strange evening – sitting in the dark with Petra, watching the screen. A story of romance unfolded, to the swoops and slides of well-played strings, and Max Black portrayed a dying businessman, hard and humourless, falling for his ditzy carer who brought sunshine to his final days. The actress was new to Rose. She had a miraculous complexion: so clean, so smooth. Rose spent the entire film wondering if it was digitally enhanced. Was anybody ever that beautiful? In comparison Max's skin looked tight, tired. But he was meant to be dying, according to the script.

Afterwards they rode the tube to Phineas's place, and sat around with him, taking three seats around a square table. Phin provided a jug of margarita.

'To us,' he said, once their frosted glasses were filled. Rose touched glasses with Phin, then with Petra, and drank.

The film was an easy place to start a conversation. Max the Object could be discussed as easily as one discusses the weather, or the decor, or the latest trash in the newspapers.

'He looked old, didn't he?' said Petra.

'Older,' Rose conceded.

'I hear he's moving into directing movies,' said Phin. 'The girl I've got guarding him now says he's working on a new project. He doesn't do anything but work. She wants a change of assignment. Says he's boring.' He smoothed a hand along his bald head. 'Even a movie star isn't enough for the young now. They want adventure. Speaking of which...'

'Yep, get down to it then, Phin,' said Petra cheerily, pouring herself more margarita.

He switched his attention to Rose alone. 'What made you want to go see that film?'

'I just wanted to,' she said, feeling defensive. 'I like silly plots. Pure escapism.' But it had been more than that – something to do with bringing two parts of her life together. She had, for the longest time, felt as if there were two halves to her that had twisted in opposite directions, like a cut peach around a stone.

And she had felt something powerful, watching Max with Petra beside her: that was definite. Max had once been all her own, and she had been his carer, his light; it had not been a concoction of the screen. Just as working with Petra was not a fabrication either. She tried to accept that she was all of these things: a bodyguard, a soldier, an investigator, a lover, a hater. Why did it matter? She didn't know.

The club was busy enough that it felt possible, even desirable, to hold an intimate conversation loudly. Or perhaps that was the margarita. 'I don't want to see him again,' she said. 'Not in person. But on the big screen, that's different. I can cope with that.'

'Whatever works,' said Petra.

'Here,' said Phin, and slid a manila folder across the table. 'Give that a look. Not here, though. I've got something else I want to talk about.'

'Really?' said Petra. 'There's a first time for everything.'

'Should I…?' Rose made a motion to stand.

'No, it's about you.'

Here it comes, she thought. The conversation she had been expecting for months, since it became obvious to her that she was no good at this life. She'd have to find a new place to live, new friends, a new person to be.

'Have you heard of EMS?'

That was a surprise. She shook her head.

Phin coughed. 'Look, it's— I don't do personal, okay, but I was reading about this EMS thing and I thought, that's Rose. Extreme Moult Syndrome. We all know some people have a bad time with it, but doctors are saying if you have to dump it all every single time then maybe it's a medical condition.'

Petra said, 'Bloody hell, they give everything a name now.'

'Look it up, that's all I wanted to tell you,' said Phin. 'Right, I'm done. Give me weekly updates on that one, it's sensitive.' He pointed at the file, then left them behind, returning to his usual seat at the bar where three men in white shirts with rolled sleeves – cardboard cutout gangsters – were waiting for him.

'I swear I don't understand him,' said Rose.

'What's to understand?'

'I just mean—'

'I reckon,' Petra said, very slowly, leaning in, 'that he has a wife somewhere in suburbia. That she calls him Graham or Keith, and he has a lawnmower and hanging baskets.'

'Really?'

'You think Phineas Spice could be his actual name?'

'But married?'

Petra shook her head. 'I'm just kidding. No, he's not married.' A change came over her expression – a decision to let the margarita move her into a confessional frame of mind. 'Listen, when I was on the Starguard books I – I had this thing with the celebrity couple I was guarding. I got attached. They didn't. He got me out of there when the time came. Sometimes I wonder if, once upon a time, he got hurt so bad that he told himself he'd never go through it again. And that's how he lives. But when he sees someone else going through it, that nearly hurts as bad, for him.'

'You think?'

She shrugged. 'It's my personal theory.'

'Is that why he took me on as a trainee investigator, after the Max thing?'

Petra winked. 'Nope. That was my idea. You think you have this EMS then? Look it up.'

'Now?'

'Come on, let's hear all about it.'

Rose checked it on her phone. There had been a documentary about it on television, a few days ago, and a website had been set up. She found a long checklist, filled with questions about behaviours: did she find it impossible to stay in contact with people after a moult? Had she ever experienced a moult after a personal trauma? Had she ever lost consciousness during a moulting? Petra replied for her as she read them aloud, saying, 'Yes, yes, yes,' until they reached the bottom, when she said, 'Well, shit,' with an air of finality.

'Yeah,' said Rose, feeling it sink into her. She had a condition. She had an explanation.

'So what's the cure?' said Petra.

'I don't think there is one. It's just an awareness thing.'

Petra raised a fist of solidarity. 'Well now we're aware.'

'I'll go see a doctor.'

'You never saw a doctor about it before?'

'Of course I did. But I don't have much luck with doctors.'

'It's not their fault being grumpy if they can't cure it. Imagine having to face a patient that you really can't help.'

'It's not my fault either. It's the way I'm made.'
'It sure is. I'm drunk.' She stated it as a fact.
'Drink less, then!'
'But that's the way I'm made,' she said, and laughed.

2013. THE COST.

'I can't help you,' I tell him. 'I'm not a proper private investigator. I never have been.'

He's reserved the whole restaurant, of course. The waitress tiptoes around me, her eyes on Max as she deposits a wicker breadbasket on the table. It's an old-fashioned bistro with a candle in a green bottle, and a padded menu with a tassle. It offers comfort food, lasagne and lamb shanks, and the promise of a dessert that won't be deconstructed. Max always did prefer this kind of food, the cheaper places with checked tablecloths, and I'm glad to see in this, at least, his tastes haven't changed.

But I haven't changed either: I always did hate eating out with him.

'I thought we'd had this conversation,' he says.

I wait until the waitress reluctantly leaves, then tell him, 'I thought I could make it work, but I can't. I was never like Petra. I wanted to be, and I suppose I thought… this time…'

'You were in love with her? Petra?'

Why would he jump to that conclusion? 'No, that's not it. It's too difficult to explain.' Impossible to explain, certainly to him.

He shakes his head and takes a white roll, dotted with little black seeds, from the basket. 'Research shows the only thing that goes with the skin is that form of sexually based attraction we call love. Nothing else. Look at the Stuck Six. They manage to all get along, still. It's beautiful to witness.'

'Yeah, I heard about them. Not in my case.'

'No, with you it's everything, isn't it? Everything gets left behind when that skin comes off. Left behind, or thrown away. Other people manage to stay friends, help each other through those dark patches. They even stay together. Why not? We don't all have to be in love.'

I've heard this before, had this argument before. 'I do. I've been diagnosed with EMS. It's who I am.'

'It is,' he says again, but this time with such quiet affection, such meaning, that I can't bear it. 'Rosie, you're unique. You think the EMS is you, and you are it. But that's not true. There's so much more to you.'

The wine is good, probably the best bottle in the whole place. I look around the room – an old habit, unnecessary, since Max has a team of three with him tonight courtesy of Starguard – and see a man standing in the alcove behind the bar behind a red curtain, half-closed. For a second I'm tense, and then I see his posture, and I know he's no threat. The manager, possibly, in deferential mode. He lifts a hand and gives me a thumbs up.

He thinks we're on a date. Everyone likes to make their own stories, for telling. For reeling out like fishing line.

Soft jazz music arrives through the speakers over the bar. The saxophone grates on my nerves.

'The Stuck Six,' I say. 'You're basing your film on the autobiography one of them wrote? I bet the rights cost a fortune.'

'It's fascinating, though, isn't it? Six people, all in love with each other at once. A miracle, some might say. You should meet Mikhael; he's the one that's been helping me with the adaptation.'

'The one that wrote the book?'

'No. The last one to fall in love.'

'The young good-looking one.' Why do I sound bitter?

'They were all young. They were all very much in love.'

'Until one of them wrote a book about it and they fell out over his version of events.'

He grimaces. 'They haven't fallen out. That was just the media talking. They're just living their own lives now. It was real, though it was different for each of them. Have you read Howard Stuck's autobiography? It's a revelation. None of us experience love in the same way, do we? I want to concentrate on that. You know their skins are in the British Museum? You can go visit them. Even touch one, if you arrange an appointment. You should. I did. It's overwhelming.'

'I'm surprised you didn't buy the bloody skins and keep them in that uncrackable safe room of yours.'

The starters arrive, just as I was gearing up to getting it all off my chest. We're sharing a wooden platter of antipasti, with gleaming meats laid next to bowls of olives, peppers, oil and vinegar. Everything on the table must be rearranged to make room for it. The candle in the bottle is moved to the next table along, so the food is in semi-darkness. It makes the music seem louder.

'Come on then,' says Max, when the waitress leaves. 'Give it to me.'

'What?'

'The reason. The real reason you don't want to work for me.'

'It's not… Look, I think you should get a proper detective. I never was. Let me go back to Lincolnshire.' Am I pleading with him now? 'I'm only good for the shop, I promise you.'

He spears an olive with a wooden pick. 'You're so wrong. And you know what? You've spent a heck of a lot of my money already. I want results.'

'I bought a skin.'

'I know.'

'I bought my skin.'

'I know!' he says, as loud and angry as I've ever seen him, flipping the platter, sending the food flying: ham, oil, everything, all over the checked tablecloth. The waitress and the manager arrive quickly, apologising – why are they apologising? They move our glasses across to the next table where our candle still burns. They fuss around, promising a new platter in only a moment. It takes so long for them to leave.

'You're an idiot,' I tell him, when I finally get the chance. 'My Max would never have done something like that.'

'It's the price I have to pay to get you to talk to me,' he says. 'For fuck's sake, Rosie, say it. I know what you bought. How mad do we both have to be before we can have the conversation?'

'You kept it.'

He flings up his hands. 'Yes! Hallelujah.'

'You kept my skin, and you promised. You promised.' I cannot allow myself to cry.

'I couldn't,' he says. 'As soon as I touched it, I knew I couldn't. I kept it – you can say no, I get it, I understand, believe me – can I have it back?'

'Not ever. Not ever.'

'Okay. Okay.'

He tries to put a hand over mine and I bat him off. 'I'm burning it. I asked you to burn it. Now I'm going to do it, and make sure it's done.'

'Okay. Have you got it here? Is it with you?'

It sits in my backpack, next to the leg of my chair. 'None of your business.'

'That's where you're wrong.'

'Why? Because you paid for it?'

'I swear,' he says, 'I swear, nobody can get under my skin the way you can. Even now.'

'It's not even whole any more.' Now I've started to speak I can't stop. 'They cut off the breasts, probably sold them separately, made a fortune. Now somebody out there owns them. Touches them.'

'What?'

'The skin, it was cut when I found out, and now I'm owned, that's owned. Some rich fan of yours is out there wearing what I felt as a fucking bra.'

'The breasts were gone.' He says the words slowly, as if inching into new territory.

'That's what I'm saying.'

'But I…' He puts his hands over his eyes. His body shakes. It takes me a moment to realise he's crying. Crying over my loss, my skin. Not his.

I can't watch him feel this as if it happened to him.

'I'm done.' I stand, pick up my backpack. 'I'll send you a report on what I learned, because that's what people in this line of work do, isn't it? But the report won't contain much, because I didn't learn much. Get someone better.'

'So you're going? That's it?' He lets his hands fall away, and the look on his face takes me back, right back, to that bathroom floor.

'Goodbye, Max.' I can't help but clutch the backpack to me as I leave the restaurant. The bodyguards, Taylor included, watch me walk away, and I don't look back.

I spend the night at a good hotel in Chichester and charge it to Max's card for no reason I can explain. I order lobster salad, drink most of the stuff in the minibar and watch an adult film, wanting him to see the itemised bill, to hold a picture in his mind of me, on this night: eating, drinking, wanking, being alive. Having a good time. Or not having a good time, depending on how he chooses to play it in his head.

He shouldn't bother me this much.

He shouldn't.

2013. **REARRANGED.**

Howard Stuck's autobiography is a thick book in a large font, with a lot of glossy pictures of the Stuck Six, from their baby photos to their posed contemporary portraits. I buy it in town for the train journey down to Bristol, and I open it at random. As I read I try to understand what Max sees in this story:

One thing I think we should all talk about more is what happens when you fall in love against your will.

Liz told me one day about the strong feelings she had always felt and rejected for an old school friend, but the attraction never came to anything, and the friend left to live with family in India. Then the friend came back, and that attraction became love. Liz said she knew it was the real emotion 'right through her skin' (those are the words she used when she told me – she always did have a beautiful way with words). She cried, I think because of the damage she was doing to us all by trying to repress those feelings, to pretend it wasn't real. Nothing ever gets improved by pretence, though, does it? That's been a hard lesson to learn.

It was a rainy Saturday night when she told me. We ordered a takeaway pizza and split the toppings, as usual: half ham and mushroom, half olives and pepperoni. Living together is about making these little compromises. And then we talked about it over a bottle of wine. I was so upset, but determined not to show it because I knew, deep down, that it wasn't her fault, or the fault of this mystery woman. I kept reminding myself of that while we ate and drank, like any normal couple would. It seemed wrong to me to have thanked the universe for the love Liz and I shared, and yet then blame anyone for the gift of more love, bestowed upon her. Didn't it mean that she was, in fact, doubly lucky? I felt certain this could be a blessing, if I could only grow as a person enough to see it in that way. Life is filled with challenges, and this was a huge one.

Liz said she didn't want to leave me, and I believed her – not just because of the fact that we were comfortable. Yes, I had a good job and it was paying for a house that she would not have been able to afford on her administrator's salary alone. Yes, if she had left me I would have been distraught, and I would have lost all the self-confidence she had given me by loving me, making me important in her eyes. Both of these considerations were true, but they weren't why I believed her. I believed her because I trusted her.

So what were my options, really? I could only see one.

I told her to be happy and to be in love with me and with this other woman. And I told her that I wanted to meet this woman, and get to know her, because I was determined that we would not split Liz into pieces, with neither of us getting the best of her. I did not want her to compartmentalise what she felt, and do damage to her spirit by splitting herself into two different people. We could be just like the pizza: many toppings, but all on one base. I remember saying that out loud (I never can hold my alcohol very well) and she laughed, and told me I was an idiot. But she was smiling, and I always did love her smile.

At that point I had no thoughts about falling in love again myself.

We finished the pizza and the wine, and went to bed. As we cuddled close I wondered how much Liz wanted this woman sexually. Was I not enough for her? These doubts ate away at me until the next day, when this threatening figure of emasculation turned up on my doorstep and turned out to be... well. She was not what I had imagined in the least.

Her name was Sunetra. She was arty and confident, with a headscarf that matched her loose, flowing red dress. She worked in computer programming although she said her heart belonged to other pursuits, like knitting, drawing, making things. She was so creative, and optimistic about life. I did not love her straight away. But I could see immediately that she was good for, and good to, Liz. Liz became alive in her presence. We sat round the kitchen table and I listened as they filled in the blanks for me, reminiscing about the past they shared. They had so many memories of being girls together, and pooling them seemed to bring them back to that innocent state, when the world was an easier place to understand.

'Do you remember Aidan?' Sunetra said to Liz, and Liz blushed and replied, 'Oh God, yes, he was so cute, we spent an entire year following him around, didn't we?'

I suddenly understood that Liz's life was a line of loves, of experiences, and I had no right to claim any of it as my own. When I began to appreciate that fact I began to love her properly, even better than I already did, and to love Sunetra too – Sunetra, a woman with her own line, her own intersections, that only at this time were parallel to my own. We would all go our separate ways again at some point, when we were done with our current skins. But not yet, I told myself. Not yet.

Things moved quickly. Within a few weeks I asked if she wanted to move in (she was having difficulties with a landlord *dispute, I remember) and she agreed. Liz was overjoyed, and love grows naturally from pleasure.*

I say naturally – I know this is a point about which many people have an opinion. How can love between three people (let alone six) be natural? Well, nature is a strange thing. If you let it run wild it strangles itself: haven't you ever noticed how weeds overpower flowers? I think what I'm really trying to say is that just because a thing is natural, doesn't mean it should grow untended.

I tended to my love for Liz, and I cultivated it. Because I did that it became easier, not harder, to fall in love again, and again, and again, and those loves never turned into a tangled mess. I made choices in the best interests of my loves, and I know the world would be a better place if we all did that.

After Sunetra moved in we began to rearrange our schedules so that we would still have time as couples as well as a three, which was, frankly, hilarious to try to organise. Looking at our diaries, sitting around that same kitchen table, pencilling in quality time – we laughed but we learned. One morning Sunetra and I got our wires crossed and ended up both turning up to a picnic for two Liz had organised at the—

I stop reading and put the book down. This oversimplified description is not a love I recognise. What kind of film will Max make of this? Is this how he rationalises what we felt for each other, with trite analogies of flowers and pizzas and growing and learning?

When the train pulls into Temple Meads I leave the book on the seat.

I grew up in Bristol. It's one of those cities that feels individual, personal, no matter how big it gets and how many smaller places it swallows up. From Temple Meads I take a taxi to the suspension bridge, and walk from there to my aunt's house. It amazes me how the bridge stays the same, no matter how many times the crew of workmen replace every single nut and bolt. The cars thunder over and the bolts shake loose, shake loose, and yet it remains somehow itself.

I suppose finding any hint of permanence in my life will always continue to surprise me.

Listen to me. Maybe deep inside, under all the skins, I'm a stand-up comedian.

The walk gets rid of the remains of my hangover. It's a bright day, warm, so Alice is probably in the garden. I ring the doorbell a few times and get no answer, so I head around the back. The garden gate is unlocked, and she has her back to it as she weeds the borders to her gravel path, kneeling upon the mat I bought her last Christmas.

'Hello Rose,' she calls, without turning around.

'You should keep this locked.'

'Why? Only you come around this way.'

'Burglars.'

'That's the job talking.'

I kneel down beside her and watch her pull out the dandelions, digging her fingers deep into the soil to reach the root. They come out white and twisted, and I think of maybe burying that old skin instead, right here. Alice would let me. But I don't ask her. Instead I say, 'I'm not an investigator any more, remember?'

'That's right. You work in a shop.' She says it without inflexion, but somehow that makes it worse.

'People change,' I say. 'They change all the time.'

She nods. I look at the pouched skin of her neck, and the way her small quick head sits upon it, as if the two don't belong together. 'Well, I'm pleased to see you anyway, even if you have changed. At least the face is the same.' She lifts her bright eyes from the ground for the first time and scans me. 'Yep, the same. Beautiful.'

'Come on,' I say, and I help her up. She's so light, as if she's down to her last skin.

The bungalow has been redecorated: painted, primped, the furniture rearranged. There are framed photographs on every wall, faces cut out in circles and grouped together to make merry collages of emotion over time. I can't help but think of all the old photos that now have head-shaped holes in them. No doubt she's kept them somewhere.

'I moulted about a month ago,' she says, 'and that pink and mauve colour scheme had to go. This is nicer, don't you think?'

I walk the length of the long wall of the living room, behind the sofa, and find some familiar faces. My dad, my mum, together. Alice has cut around them with irregular sweeps of the scissors, giving them strange curves. Dad moulted only a few months after Mum got pregnant with me but I saw them both regularly throughout my childhood. They remained polite, if not exactly friends; I think this is the first time I've seen them captured as a couple in an image.

Alice is on the wall, young and free, snipped to stand next to nobody. She has lived in this house for so many years, only feeling the need to change the paint and the position of the furniture when she changes her skin. If she's had lovers they have come and gone unknown to me.

'How are you feeling?' I ask her.

'Fine. A bit of a sore shoulder. Doctor Whitmore said less gardening, give it a chance to rest.' She shrugs, and looks cheeky and guilty and shamefaced, all at once, like a child. 'You can tell me off, it's fine. I won't mind.'

'No thanks. If you can't be bothered to look after yourself...' Then I realise that's just another parental trick, the long-standing alternative to the classic telling off, so I don't finish the sentence.

'You're here for the skin,' she says. 'The first one of yours. Aren't you?'

'How did you know?'

'I wish you wouldn't take it. I can take good care of it. Your mum asked me to, when she got diagnosed. It was very precious to her.'

'I know, but I can't. I need to know it's gone. Done with. What made you think I'd want it?' It seems such a leap of intuition.

She brushes her cheek with her fingers, an old nervous gesture of hers. 'Someone phoned, a few hours ago, and they were offering quite a bit of money for young female skins, they said. They were quite insistent about it and the price kept going up, and I just got this feeling, like they knew there was one in the house and they wanted that one in particular. I thought, afterwards, I bet Rose turns up looking for that old skin. I don't know why.'

'You got the feeling that someone wanted my old skin and you didn't tell me, and you're still swanning around in the back garden with the gate unlocked?' She's so unaware at times I could scream.

She gets up from her favourite armchair, which has been moved to the other side of the room since my last visit.

'You're here now anyway, aren't you? You're going to take it no matter what I say. Here.' From underneath the television cabinet she pulls out a brown paper package, flat and square and tied with string. 'See? Nobody would have looked there.'

'That's not the point.' I take the package and am glad it's wrapped up tight. Who wants to touch their teenage mind once more?

'Anybody would think you were the grand old lady,' she mutters, 'the way you nag.'

'Just— I'll feel better if you lock the gate. And if you get another phone call, will you let me know? Straight away?' She nods. I put the package in my bag, next to the other skin, and close the zip. 'Did they say anything about who they were? On the phone?'

'Not really. Money Moult, maybe? Not one of those from the television. It was a man. A nice voice. He called me by name.'

'Alice?'

'Mrs Stacey. He had a posh accent. Upper class.'

'All right.' Maybe it really was just a fishing phone call from one of those companies. They can be pushy, particularly with the elderly, who always seem to have old skins squirreled away. It's one thing to burn your own moults, but the first moult of your child – that seems to be an entirely different matter. That's the Bond. So much stronger than love, the way a parent feels about a child, that's what the stories say. The Bond is the only eternal attachment; I read that somewhere.

'Listen,' says Alice. 'When your mum and I were little, our mum – your Gran Stacey – told us that shedding was a necessary thing we all have to do to take away the bad thoughts. She said we all feel better afterwards, and it only removes the things that should go. Love, the romantic stuff, that's just a trick to make you make babies. It's not meant to last. But other things are. The Bond is. It's not skin deep. The people you meet, and love, and,' she purses her lips, 'have relations with, they're here today, gone tomorrow. But family isn't. Look at us, we get along, don't we? And that's just a shadow of the Bond, from aunt to niece. Come and move in here, and if you find someone to love then love them, and let them go. Maybe even make a baby with them, and we can take care of it. Then you'll know what forever means, Rose. It means a child.'

'Until they turn into a teenager and get their first moult.' I peruse the walls once more. I don't like this conversation, and we've had it often enough before. She was never brave enough to have a baby and now she wants me to do it for her. But that first peeling away – the absolute need I felt to escape my mother and her consuming, eternal need for me – I don't want to experience that from the other side. How I hurt her, when I left.

Alice returns to her armchair, stiff with age and indignation. 'It doesn't affect every child the way it affected you.'

'So I might get lucky, is that it?'

She shakes her head. It strikes me that she looks like me. Or, rather, I will look like her, one day. Alone, in my own bungalow, with weeds to pull and young faces on the wall.

'Do you wish you'd done it, now?' I ask her. 'Had a baby, I mean?'

'Of course,' she says, but now I find, hearing her say the words, that I don't quite believe her. She's still scared of it.

'It's just nature. The Bond. You said it yourself. A way to make babies get born, and cared for longer than just one skin.'

'It's all just nature,' she says, her tone brusque. 'What difference does it really make to any of us, whether it's natural or not? You worry about the strangest things.'

I've annoyed her, I can tell. Coming to visit her always does end in annoyance, on one side or the other. Usually both.

I find my own face, small and grainy, in a large clip-frame of many cut-out people. I look very young. Next to me, tilted so that the sides of our heads are touching, is a glossy photo snipped from a magazine. It's Max. Max's professional, smiling face.

I point at it. 'What's this?'

'What?'

'You know very well what.'

She sniffs. 'It's my wall. I'll put what I like on it.'

'Take it down.'

'Rose,' she says, in her reasonable voice. 'He belongs there. He was the love of your life.'

So we have an argument, which is, I think, what we both wanted.

After the argument we pass another hour in silence, watching quiz shows on television and eating biscuits from the tin. Then we make up wordlessly, as families do, and she says she'll drive me to Clifton's Public Incinerator, if that's what I really want.

As families do.

> • <

How I hate car journeys…

There's a long queue at the Incinerator, the cars moving slowly, people taking their time to drive up to the chute that leads to the flames. The machine is transparent so you can watch the voyage of your old skin as it slides down to go up in smoke. The authorities leave no room for doubt. You see it destroyed with your own eyes.

Alice sighs beside me. The radio is playing old songs and she hums along, knowing maybe one word in ten, mumbling at the rest.

With the heat of the afternoon sun hitting my side of the car, and the music at work upon me, I can't help but think the worst thoughts. The things I saw that will never go away, no matter how matter times I shed, no matter what Alice tells me about Gran Stacey's old sayings. The skins discarded or taken by force; the sweat and the smell of bad people doing bad things; the empty shining of the studio lights on Max, making him seem a little bigger, a little flatter, like nothing more than a white smile that had nothing to do with me. The bathroom floor. Then playing at being detective, and the warehouse in Slough, next to a patch of scrubland, the people driving by.

Being a private investigator wasn't about helping people. I realise now that I wanted to know how bad this world can be, and I got an answer. I found basements and gambling rings and hospitals and cemeteries, and so many ways to buy and belittle love. To cut it, to measure, sew it and dress it and grind it up small and put it in those endless lines of pills.

I know why Max keeps buying the pills. It's an act of optimism, and I can't blame him for that. He never sees the worst of the world. So many people are employed to keep it from him, and the rest happily do it for free because of who he is and what his handsome face on the screen gives to them all. That moment of escape from reality.

We're nearing the front of the queue. The two brown paper packages sit in my lap. Shall I open them, touch them one last time? The thing that stops me is the mutilation that was performed upon one of them: the removal of the breasts and the sewing up of the slits. It's the thought of someone else touching it, cutting it, that is too hard to bear. The thought of someone profiting from my skin, although it makes no sense that it was mutilated as the price would have been so much better for the complete skin. And nobody would have been fooled to think it was a male skin, not for more than a few seconds. The seller had to know that.

Max's face, when he learned about the removal of the breasts. I don't think I've ever seen him so surprised.

There it is.

The thing I should have worked out straight away.

I know who took my skin, and Max's skins. But I don't know why.

We reach the front of the queue and the open mouth of the incinerator chute is on the driver's side of the car. Alice winds down her window and holds out her hands.

'Come on, then.'

I shake my head.

'Are you doing it or not, Rose?'

'Not,' I say, sounding like a child. Like nothing more than a baby.

'Right.' She sets off, through the gateway, and I can't tell if she's pleased or not. We travel for a few miles before she says, 'So what will you do with them?'

'Would you keep the old one? My first one?'

'I was doing that anyway.'

'I know. Thanks.'

She hums along to the latest song on the radio for a moment. It's a ballad I've not heard before about how the shortest love is the sweetest love, and a day together is better than a lifetime alone. Then she says, 'Do I still need to make sure the back gate is locked to protect your precious skin?'

'You should do that anyway. But no, I don't think anyone is bothered about it now. Or, at least, they won't be. I'll sort it.'

'I don't like the sound of that.'

'I'm sorting it,' I repeat. 'Then I'll come visit. For longer. When it's done.'

She considers this, her eyes on the road, then says, 'Don't end up like me, Rose. Don't end up alone. I know you have this thing, this moulting problem and it makes you want to leave everything behind because it hurts so much, but try to hold on to something. You don't always have to be the one that leaves.'

I don't say anything. I feel her words sinking into me and I hate it, I hate it. If it was a choice I would have already decided to be different. I would scratch this out of my skin myself if I could.

'Can you drop me at the station?' I ask her.

'I thought we were going home! The station's in the other direction.'

'Then I suppose it's time to perform a U-turn,' I say, and I catch, on the side of her face, the flicker of a smile.

PART TWO

2008. **SPOONFUL.**

Petra's car was one of those contract jobs, set up to be changed every seven years or with a new skin; some customers liked that freedom, although it sounded more like a flashy extension to an existing jail block to Rose. This car or that car: the deal remained the same.

But Petra said she liked her green Volvo, and had felt no need to change it after her last moult. The back seat was piled high with discarded bottles and wrappers, and the large boot was crammed with electronic devices and more traditional methods of applying brute force. The camera zooms and the hammers, all mixed up together; it was a wonder nothing got cracked.

As they drove along, silent in the early morning, it occurred to Rose that this was a car worthy of Mary Poppins, and it amused her to think of Petra, so capable, so practically perfect in every way, in that role. She hummed 'A Spoonful of Sugar' under her breath as the low sun began to gain in strength.

'Really?' said Petra, 'Musical numbers? You kept that quiet.'

They stopped at a service station, drank lattes in tall

glasses and ate doughnuts, choosing one table at random from a sea of them. It was early enough to feel that the place was theirs, and the few people who came and went were just passing through their territory. Men in suits, mainly, getting ahead of the game. Rose watched them stride to and from the blue signs of the toilet block, or order takeaway coffee from the dark wood and chrome counter, and wondered if each one was neck deep, drowning in some terrible form of business. Skin business.

All skin business was terrible, she had decided, from the creams and salves to the cutting and slicing. Inescapable and everywhere, looking like a quiet man in a suit, going about his day, until she looked closer.

'We're just checking this place out,' said Petra, skimming the milk foam from the rim of the glass with her finger and licking it clean. 'It's off all the books. I reckon it's a holding place for skins this guy is trying to move on the side. We get a few photos of the product and the setup, give them to Phin, and then Phin has leverage.'

'Right.'

'It's straightforward.'

'Yep.'

'Great,' said Petra. 'So you can do it then. I'll wait in the car.'

Rose had suspected it was building to this. 'What if I get caught?'

'Easy answer to that one: don't get caught.' The foam had been licked clean; Petra picked up the glass and drained it. 'Look, it's a warehouse on the outskirts of Slough at six in the morning. There's going to be nobody there. You keep your hood up in case of security cameras, you take a few photos, you leave. You don't take anything, and if it doesn't feel right you walk away. I wouldn't drop you straight in the deep end. This is a long-term training process. One step at a time.'

Rose sipped her coffee. 'But why train me?'

Petra sighed. 'I keep telling you, I fancied some company.'

Recently she had begun to feel a vexation building in the older woman, transmitting itself in the way Petra moved around the office, asking questions and seeming unhappy with the answers. Rose suspected she was disappointed in her.

'I am trying,' Rose said.

'I know. It's fine.'

'I enjoy the work.' Which was true, although the part she enjoyed was the moment when each case could be called over. The burning of the manila file, the ritual of it, pleased her beyond words.

'Do you ever wonder if you would have been better off staying with Max?'

'How could I? You know about my condition.'

'Yeah. Your condition, I know. But people do, all sorts of people. They just pretend to still love someone, after that skin comes free. Not just for a comfortable life, although in your case I could have understood it. To live in that world.'

'That's world's not real.' Honesty prompted her to add, 'Nothing is, though, is it?'

'This is,' said Petra, and pinched her hand.

'Ow!'

'Snap out of it. I know you still check up on him. You read the gossip columns. You watch all the movies. You still have feelings for him.'

'I really don't.'

'That's you all over. It's only real when you say it is.'

'What do you want me to say?'

'I want you to really commit to this life,' snapped Petra. 'I'm going to the loo. Think about what you're going to do. You're going to get into that warehouse and take those photos, and when you come out of the warehouse you'll be a tiny amount closer to being a proper private investigator.'

After she had gone Rose took a sugar cube from the bowl and crunched it. The sweet shards of the cube dissolved in her mouth to nothing, so quickly, so she ate another and sucked it this time, trying to make it last.

2013. SEWN UP.

Back at the Sussex mansion the weather is not right for filming, so Max has given everyone the day off. The gate guard – not Mike this time but an unfamiliar face – tells me that lots of them organised themselves into cars and left for London. Others are ensconced in their trailers, no doubt moaning or playing cards or swapping tips about skin treatments, as actors do.

But Max – Max is in his home, and Taylor is nowhere to be seen.

'You're not meant to be left unprotected,' I say. It seems there's a little bit of the bodyguard left in me after all.

'I sent her out,' he says. 'On an errand.'

'Dry cleaning?'

'Listen, I don't want to discuss who does what for me any more. I just want one final thing from you. That's the only reason I agreed to let you in.'

We are standing in his living room, on the dark wooden floor. He is nervous; his hands move over the material of his jeans, stretched tight over his thighs.

'One final thing,' I echo.

'The skin. The skin I paid a fortune for.'

It's that sinking realisation that I was right. I was right about him, oh God, I was right. I didn't realise how much I was hoping I was mistaken until I heard those words.

'It's my skin,' I say, carefully.

'I paid for it.'

'I'll pay you back.'

'With what? With the money you earn in that place in the middle of nowhere, with that teenager hoping you'll take pity on him and fuck him? You could never afford it, and you know it, so don't bullshit me, Rosie. Have more respect for me than that.'

'Stay calm,' I tell him.

'I'm calm. Give me the skin.'

'I can't.'

'Why not?' He is so tense, his hands rubbing at the denim. 'Have you burned it?' It's as if his world could turn on my answer.

I shake my head.

The tension seeps out of him, through his shoulders and his hands. 'Oh thank God,' he says. 'Thank God. I had to know. I had to know if you could do it.' He bends over at the waist and takes in long deep breaths.

'If it's so important to you, why did you let someone steal it?' I ask him.

Slowly, he straightens. He locks his gaze on mine. 'I don't know what you're talking about.'

A line.

'I'm guessing your own skins never left this house,' I venture. 'Probably back in your safe room by now, locked up tight. Am I right?'

'You're crazy. I lost them all.'

'Is that so? I saw your face when you heard my skin had been mutilated. That was the shock, for you. Nothing else. That was all you cared about.'

He raises an eyebrow at me, and that gesture pushes me into action. I run from the living room, down the hall, and take the steps two at a time to his safe room in the basement. The door is open, as is the wardrobe.

Hanging within are a selection of light summery dresses

in many colours. And next to them, touching them, are his skins.

I hear him close the door behind me, the sliding of a bolt, and I know in that split second that I never have been, and never ever will be, a proper investigator. I am an idiot, and he knew it, right from the beginning. He knew it. I look at the door, and see his face through a slot that has been made in the wood. He was having renovations done, when I first came. He had a plan in place.

'The pills by the bed,' he says. 'Take them.'

The room has been decorated, turned into a bedroom for one: a single divan, a small table on its right and an upholstered chair, green, on its left. A black and white photograph, large, framed, hangs over the bed; it's that shot of Paris again. That dream of Paris. The bedside table holds a plastic jug of water with a matching glass, and two pink pills.

'Let me out,' I say. 'This isn't funny.'

'Take the pills and I'll let you out.'

And I think – why not? The pills never worked. The endless pills.

I cross to the bed, quick, and swallow them down, without water. 'There. Let me out.'

'Oh Rosie,' he says. 'There's nobody like you.' He closes the slot in the door.

I call out. I hammer on the door. Eventually I start shredding his skins; millions of pounds and memories, turned to strips with each touch reminding me of how good he once was. But he doesn't come back, and I'm only halfway through destroying the third skin when the pills kick in and take the world away.

> • <

My skin is loose.

I feel it, feel it slipping from me, separating out from the layer beneath.

It's too early. I should have years yet, but that itch, that building itch, I know it. Intense and innate. I move to scratch, and as I dig my nails into my stomach and thighs, finding the skin there already hard and white, I look around the room and place myself with it. It used to be the safe room, and now it's my personal prison, complete with bed, sink, and pictures of trees in blossom, the Eiffel Tower rising above them, on the wall.

He's been planning this from the start.

'I'm sorry,' he says, close by, above me.

I'm lying on the floor. I'm naked. I'm naked, and I can see him now, sitting on the bed only a few feet away, looking not at my face but at my hands as I scratch. He is fully dressed, in a different shirt from the last time I saw him.

How long was I unconscious?

The itching has turned into pain – needles under the skin. I can't scratch long enough, deep enough. I can't think any more.

'No,' he says, over and over, and he moves to me and pins down my hands. 'Not so hard, Rosie, not so hard.'

'The induced moulting will make it painful,' says a different voice, a woman. I've heard that voice before. 'Sedation's an option, but it can affect the emotional transfer.'

Max frowns. I dig my nails into his hand and he flinches, but he doesn't let go. I'm on fire, knock me out, take me away. Everything is alight.

'I need her to let it all go. To be clean.'

'Restraints, then. Can you manage?'

'Taylor,' he calls, and another voice replies, 'Yep.' I don't see her, but I think she's at my ankles. Max grabs me under my arms and together they take me to the bed, and then hold me down as my wrists and ankles are placed in the prepared restraints.

'How long?' says Max.

'At least overnight,' says the disembodied voice.

'Christ,' he says. He is unhappy. I need to scratch. I twist and turn, and rub myself against the sheet upon the mattress.

What do I love? What will I lose, this time?

Nothing.

That thought reassures me. I love nobody, have loved nobody and nothing since my last moult. I have nothing important to lose.

I laugh.

I can't stop.

'Get out,' says Max. Then he sits beside me as I laugh and squirm, and lose myself all over again.

> • <

I am here, and I am whole.

My latest moult is nowhere to be seen. I can't remember the act of shedding it. I'm no longer in restraints, either. My wrists bear two red circles, like bracelets, but the marks don't hurt. I wonder if I'll wear them throughout this skin.

I feel—

I don't know what I feel.

Max is not here. I get up and walk around the room, in circles, for a while. I pour myself a glass of water from the bedside table, and savour it in my throat, and then I get the feeling that I'm not alone.

The eyes are watching me through the slot in the door. My first response is to throw the glass at them, but it's plastic, I forgot. The plastic simply bounces off, and the water splashes over the floor.

The eyes return.

They are brown, and in this letterbox form they are empty of any expression I can read. They are rimmed by thick orange glasses.

'Sit on the bed please,' says Anna Mallory.

'Where's Max?'

'He's gone for some rest. He was exhausted. He watched over you for days.'

'Days?'

'This is for the best. We're going to help you. With your condition.'

There are so many things I could say to that, but I think carefully, and settle for a question instead. 'Why?'

'No doubt Max will want to explain it. He'll be here in a moment. If you'll sit on the bed and wait, please.'

Footsteps ring down the corridor.

'Bed, please,' she repeats, and I retreat to it.

The door opens and then Max is here, looking tired and dishevelled and movie-starrish. It's in the way he holds his head; this is a moment he's rehearsed. Anna and Taylor enter after him.

'She's awake,' he says, over his shoulder, to his audience.

'She's fine,' says Anna. 'Good to go.'

'You sure you can do this?'

'Nothing is risk free. But this is what we've been working for all these years, right?'

That seems to reassure him. He steps towards me and I shrink back; it's an automatic reaction, but one that gives him that disappointed look.

'Okay,' he says. I don't know if it's to me or to Anna. 'Let's do it.'

'Rose, I'm going to sedate you again. Are you going to let me, or shall we hold you down? It's up to you.' She has that medical manner – *This is for your own good* is written through her.

If I open my mouth I would beg, and say all the things that desperate people say. So I say nothing. If I don't say it, then I can't be here. It can't be true.

She comes to me, and injects me just over the crook of my elbow, and the new skin is so soft that the needle glides in easily, like a friend, invited.

> • <

My name is Rose Allington.

My name is Rosie Allington.

Max is holding my hand. I smile at him, and he smiles back, and then I realise I can't breathe properly. My skin is suffocating; it has been sewn up tight into a sack that I can't escape. It presses up against my legs, my arms, my stomach, my head. It adheres to my cheeks and nose and forehead, and to the edges of my mouth.

My hands and feet are tied to the bed once more. Max is sweaty.

'Hey,' he says. 'You gave me a scare. We nearly lost you. The anaesthetic, we think.'

'Don't be scared,' I say, to me and to him. I don't want either of us to suffer any more. 'Just help me. Help me take this off.'

'But it's working,' he whispers.

The pressure is stifling. I lift my head from the pillow and look down the length of my body. I'm not clothed. Yes I am. I'm stitched into a skin. My own, used skin. The skin that loved him.

Two diamond patches are missing over the breasts; I can see my own nipples. They have a reality that everything else in this room does not. They are mine.

'I couldn't get them back, Rosie,' he says, squeezing the dead skin that is wrapped around my hand. 'I've made them pay for it though. That was never part of the deal, but no, they had to try to get even richer. These people are scum. That's why I phoned your aunt, put on a phony accent, tried to get an earlier skin of yours so I could at least replace what was missing, but no dice.'

'You should have burned it,' I say. My lips tickle.

'I could say the same to you. But you didn't, did you? I had to know if you could. I figured, if you were prepared to track my skins down, and if you couldn't burn your love for me when you got the chance, that you'd want me – deep down – to go ahead with this. To make you better. Make you happy again.'

'Love?'

'Yes. You can love me again. Like I still love you. I'm still in the same skin, Rosie. I'm here in the same skin.'

I shake my head, and hear the dead skin crackle against the pillow. 'No, you're different.'

'I funded Mallory Peace. I heard about Anna, and the breakthroughs she'd made, and I set her up in business. I've been taking their pills since the beginning, and they work. The pills work. I'm still the same person I was. The person you loved.'

But my love, the memory of it stitched tight around me like a shroud, says otherwise.

'No,' I say. 'You're not.'

He frowns. He lets go of my hand.

'It takes time,' says Anna Mallory, unseen by me. She's close by. 'The new skin takes roughly seventy-two hours to become impregnated by the old skin.'

'But she's suffering!' he says.

I concentrate on each breath as they argue. This pressure on my chest; it's not the skin. It's dead love.

> • <

'Do you like this room? I had it decorated for you. I thought you'd like it. It's always the first thing you notice, isn't it, Rosie? How a room is decorated.'

'No it's not,' I say, but he's right. I've never noticed it before. I'm always checking out the room: the positioning of objects, the angle of the furniture, as if it means something. I've done it all my life.

'You used to hate that fish tank I owned, do you remember? You said it made the place look like a drug baron's palace. I suppose that's what I am, now, in a way. But it's for you.

Working on a cure, for you.'

'I don't want to be cured.'

But he talks on, as if he can talk love back into me.

'Remember when we met?' he says. 'I loved you straight away. I never told you that before because I knew you'd laugh at me.'

He has created a scene of it in his head. He played one character, and I played the other. But he didn't love me straight away. He looked me up and down and said to Phineas Spice, 'That's fine.' I wasn't even a she to him then. I was that. And I liked it, to be an object of business. He was certainly an object of business for me, right up until Paris.

Paris sneaks from my old skin to the new. I feel it permeating me. If he mentions Paris he will see that emotion in my eyes, and I don't want to give him that. I want to hurt him, this stranger who hurts me while wearing that familiar face. The face that never did love me straight away, no matter what the mouth says.

He talks on. 'You made a list.'

'Of what?'

'Of your skins.' He pulls a piece of notepaper from his pocket. 'I found it in your backpack, with the skin. A list of all the times you changed, and you never told me. You never would tell me.'

I picture myself on that train; why do I always seem more complete in the past? My concerns, my thoughts, were solid on the train, sitting in that forward facing seat with the slice of early morning sunlight falling on the sticky tabletop. Already it seems an age ago.

'Age sixteen. First moult,' he reads.

'Yes.'

'I want to know what it was like. I've always wanted to know.'

'I never wanted to – it wasn't about hurting you.' I can't bear the thought of his pain. It must be working, this process, this sewing up into old skin.

'You've been protecting yourself,' he says. 'But there's no need, now.'

I laugh at that. And the funniest part is his hurt expression; he really doesn't see it.

'Sixteen. You were sixteen years old. Tell me.'

'It's none of your business.'

'I'm in love with you,' he says, as if that explains everything. 'What do I have to do to make you believe that? I'll tell you about my first moult.'

'I know about that.'

'I didn't tell you everything. Listen. I was in Manhattan. My father's apartment. He was away on a shoot, and I was watching a movie.'

'I know,' I repeat. 'One of the movies he'd directed. It triggered something. You told me before.' I'm ashamed to say I'm bored of it.

'It wasn't one of his. I lied. It was a dirty movie. I was whacking off when I got that itchy feeling, all over.' His eyes are on my stomach, on the join where the skin has been sewn up around me. 'The skin came off in my hand. The skin on my dick.' He shrugs and blushes, like a little boy. 'I screamed. The maid came running. Found me that way.'

'Why wouldn't you tell me that?'

'It's hardly flattering.'

'Does that matter?' But my real problem is that I much prefer the other version of the story, when his father the famous director makes a film that leads to a reaction in his only neglected son. It has more pathos. This story is ridiculous – the story of the maid and the boy caught with his trousers round his ankles. It suits him less.

'Your turn,' he says, with a cheeky smile. 'You were sixteen years old.'

Oh, Max. What a creation he is.

'I was sixteen years old,' I say, and the words come from that start, and flow from the memory. There I am again, the solid me of the past. The one version of myself I can understand.

1986. THE FIRST TIME.

'Mine wasn't that bad,' said her mother from the seat beside her. 'It just came right off. I don't understand it.'

All emotion had left Rose since her first moult, but here they were, back in a sudden rush; she hated her mother, she hated her, she hated her, the loud voice, the drone of it, the fact that her mother could discuss such an intensely personal thing in front of a collection of strangers in a doctor's waiting room. And the strangers: she hated them too. Listening and pretending not to, hearing and not really caring either way.

The open-plan stretch of the waiting room from sliding double doors to reception desk was light and airy. Rows of chairs were bookended with small pine tables bearing magazines, and people sat in their own patterns, leaving spaces where one group ended and another began.

Her mother had chosen the front row, before a large poster. Block lettering listed the warning signs of serious skin conditions, from misshapen moles to constant itching.

'At least it came off in one,' said her mother. 'But it took so long, and you don't look right. I think we really should just get you checked out.'

Shut up, Rose said in her head. Shut up.

'Soon be over and done with.' The pat of her mother's hand on her knee appalled her; she couldn't help but flinch.

'Is it still tender?'

Unable to raise her eyes, Rose nodded.

'Rose.'

There was no escape. She had to look up, and meet her mother's eyes. Why was it unbearable, to see and be seen this way? She felt as if she had lost herself, sloughed off every emotion that made her who she was. In its place, fast expanding to take up the emptiness, was black, viscose hatred of everyone who had ever lost their skin and thought it no big deal.

She stood up, and walked fast. Walked away.

Her mother called her name. Rose's walk turned into a run.

> • <

'You made up with her, right? Your mom?'

'Of course. It was just… I don't know. The triggering of the disease. But it didn't affect the Bond for long. The Bond is different.'

I don't need to say that it was never quite the same, though, do I?

'So that's why,' he muses. 'Why you ended up working for that Skin Disease Clinic in Lincoln. To make up to your mom. On some level.'

That's too neat and tidy. It's ridiculous.

'This EMS, it makes you want to push everyone away. You can see that, right? It needs a cure. Think how many people we can help, if we get it right. With you,' he says.

I close my eyes.

The thing is it feels good, to tell it, to talk of it, and to have his verdict, his summation. Why should that help? It's almost an act of erasure. It takes out so much of what I've felt and discards it as unimportant. Simply a part of my illness.

And if Max does manage to remove the illness, what will be left?

> • <

He feeds me tangerine. The dead skin pulls at my neck as I lift my head for each segment. After that sweetness there are more pills to swallow, and if I take them without a fuss he smiles. I feel better, when I see him smile.

Afterwards, I say, 'You're hurting me.'

Still smiling, he says, 'It can't be worse than how you hurt me.'

'It's revenge, then.'

'No, it's not that. That's not part of it.'

'How can you be so sure?'

'Because I'm giving you a gift.'

My new skin, underneath, has been rubbed and rubbed by the old. It's as tender as a blister. But my breasts, they remain free. I focus on my nipples; on the air upon them.

'Tell me about Steve. Your first love. You were twenty-one.'

'I was twenty-one,' I repeat. Steve, who moulted me off.

'You got kicked out of college for him.'

'University. And I wasn't kicked out because of him.' Not exactly.

'So tell me how it was.'

1991. **STARTING A FIRE.**

Rose folded her skin up small, and put it at the bottom of the metal bin.

It was late. Most of the students were out, drinking and clubbing. She had gone to the pub and drunk too much without feeling it, telling everyone she had just moulted and it had been fine. An easy one. But back here, in her room with its single bed, single desk, single chair, lone Dalí poster covering cracked paint, she couldn't pretend. Her hands were clumsy. It took her four attempts to light a match.

Steve no longer loved her. Well, she no longer loved him, so that made them equal. All the love had seeped out of her with this moult, and now she was clean and new – emptied of love. Yet the memory of him saying – I've shed, this can't work any more – hurt so much. She couldn't understand it. She never wanted to touch the skin that had loved him again.

It caught quickly. It crackled. She fed the fat little flame of it, fed it photographs of the two of them, then the poems he had written for her:

Our skins entwine
and rub
and bleed together
so our love sinks deeper
deeper to the bones
the bones
and beyond

It deserved to burn; all the untrue, stupid sentences of the world should burn. She hoped he was burning the things she had written to him, those long letters telling him every thought that came to her, every feeling she had experienced about her life so far. And when the fire began to die she fed it her lecture notes, her painstakingly careful handwriting on the subject of Ancient Greece, she gave those to the fire too, and felt better, and better, with each lick of heat along the sharp white edges, curling them over, twisting them to ash.

I'm not a child any more, Rose thought. I will never give away so many secrets about myself again.

Then she pictured the days ahead. The days of building up emotions only to have them crumble away with each moult. The lovers who would be taken away. The husband, maybe. One day she would wake and find she had left him behind, and she hadn't even met him yet.

She reached for the bottle of vodka, a quarter empty, and tipped liquid freely over the flames. The flames followed the trail, leaping up to the bottle. She dropped it as an automatic reaction; the flames began to spread across the carpet and she knew in that moment she had gone too far, that she still wanted all those days and lovers ahead even if they could not last forever.

She stumbled from the room, screamed 'Fire!' up the stairwell, ran to the lobby and dialled 999 on the payphone as a few students emerged from their rooms, sniffing at smoke. They filed past her as she gave their address, and wearily began to assemble on the pavement opposite the hall of residence.

When she joined them, their expressions seemed to say to her: if it's not one thing, it's another.

How adult they all were, now. How boring it was, to feel.

> • <

'How much longer?' I whisper.

'Not long.'

'I smell.'

Max laughs a little. 'Yes,' he says, 'you do. Once we get you out of that old skin you can have a good long bath. How do you feel?'

That's a difficult question to answer. I understand him better. I've seen his desperation to reel back time, to make us what we were again. I care about him, I do. I don't know if that's the fault of the process, or of being kept here; could it be some sort of Stockholm syndrome? Whatever it is, it's making me hate myself a little more every minute.

'Fine,' I say. 'You look tired, though.'

'I feel like we're getting somewhere, and I can't sleep for thinking about it,' he admits.

'Do you still hate to be touched?'

'I don't hate it. I just prefer to be the one doing the touching. Tell me about Cyprus.'

'The third moult.'

'You were twenty-eight years old.'

'I was in the RAF. But it wasn't how you think.'

'Did you see action?.'

'No, Cyprus isn't— It wasn't… I was… I was…'

1998. HEAT.

Rose was a soldier second and an administrator first: working on the logistical side, ordering supplies, marking movements on maps. She knew how to use a gun and could run five miles in forty minutes, but mainly she could use a computer and keep a lot of other people running in the right direction.

The poster behind her desk bore a quote from Frederick the Great:

An Army Marches on its Stomach.

And so she was organised. An organised, proper person.

When she felt the first signs of her time approaching she informed her CO and got signed off for two days, then checked herself into the Moulting Ward.

It was an issue of temperature; the heat could cause problems in moulting for people who weren't used to it. The ward was temperature controlled, and it was pleasant to sit in the communal area, listening to British Forces Radio, feeling the itch build.

A Flight Lieutenant she didn't know came in, and they chatted for a while about home and family, but his moult was moving faster than hers. He left for a private cubicle to get the process over with, and then the overhead strip lights kicked in as day dimmed outside the window.

Why was it taking so long?

She was a woman now, grown, doing a job; she was responsible. It had been seven years since the last moult, so the timing was right. The stress of getting accepted into the RAF, training, being posted overseas: none of those had triggered a moult. And this time there was no Steve, no love to be lost. She wanted it done with, gone in a day. She wanted to prove how easy this process could be.

Forces Radio closed down for the night, and still there was only the itch.

At some point during the dark hours a member of the medical staff put her head around the door and looked surprised to see Rose still sitting there.

'Go get some sleep in one of the private cubicles,' she suggested, but Rose shook her head. She couldn't face a small white space, or a medical bed with the sheets pulled tight, if it wasn't about to happen.

'It's a quiet night,' said the medical officer, and left.

Slowly, the itching intensified.

Rose dozed in one of the new plastic stackable chairs that had been flown out from home; she had put through the order herself. So many things here in Cyprus had been transported, hundreds of miles, to make this recognisable, to ground the troops in familiarity.

A sharp sting pierced her lower back. She jerked up from the chair and touched the sore spot through her uniform. The skin was pouching out, heavy with liquid. Not an insect bite, then, but a new facet of the moult. The thought triggered a realisation: the itching had become pain. She was in pain, all over, but strong on her back and buttocks, and it was growing, this pain; it would eat her up. Wherever it touched the skin puffed, as if injected with it, and the lights were too bright, the uniform too rough. She couldn't stay here.

Rose walked out of the communal area and passed the medical officer in the corridor, who threw her a quizzical look, but said nothing. She walked on, out of the building, into the night air, so clean – and then the urge swept over her to run.

Running through the dark, quiet base, she imagined running right out of her skin, leaving it behind as a ghostly outline. The green buildings passed by, all the same, big as barns, holding sleeping soldiers, and she accelerated, outstripping the urge to be counted as one of them. She no longer wanted to belong.

To belong – why should that emotion abandon her?

Belonging was a form of love, perhaps.

The perimeter of Akrotiri base was demarcated by a tall fence. Rose reached it, pressed her face to the holes, and willed herself through, as if she could be poured from her skin on to the rocky ground beyond, and from there to the sea. The uniform held her back. She stripped it off, and the night air was so cold, so cold.

Lights swung down upon her; a voice said, 'Stay still, stay still.' She reached through the fence but only her fingers would fit. The pain redoubled and her skin was loose upon her. She wriggled free of it, not caring who was watching, then tried to bury it in the dusty ground. She dug with a frenzy.

'Christ,' said a thick voice, disgusted by her. She didn't care. A blanket was placed around her shoulders. More lights arrived, and she was lifted, taken to one of the identical buildings, and a bed.

The next day the RAF began the process of ejecting her from their ranks as a liability. It was fine. Her urge to be there had vanished, and all that was left was shame that she had ever wanted to take part in the first place.

> • ‹

'I thought you were this hard woman,' says Max. 'A killer.'

'I pushed paper for a while.'

'Did Phineas Spice know? That you were an administrator?'

'It never came up in conversation.'

Max laughs.

I can't help but wonder how he could have known me, held me, and thought me a killer? Didn't the truth of me shine through?

'What is it about me that you love?' I ask him.

How odd it is to be having this conversation. I should scream and cry, and he should say scary things about what he'll do to me if I don't at least try to love him back. That's how captors and captives speak.

'You want a list?' he says.

Those wide, playful eyes take me back to the tone we used to stretch between us, like a net in a game.

'Yeah, I want an actual list. To make up for the list you stole from my bag.'

'Right then.'

'Come on then. Don't tell me you have to think about it.'

'You're unique. I've told you that before.'

'You're wrong. But okay.'

'You make me feel cared for,' he says.

I don't correct him, although he has to know he should say it in the past tense.

'You're so beautiful.'

I lie still, sewn up, knowing I am anything but. There's no need to reply to this one either.

'You give it meaning,' he tells me.

'What?'

He wets his lips, then says, 'My life. You give my life meaning.'

'How do I do that?'

'I don't know. It's just one of your many mysterious talents, which now, apparently, include running away from doctors and hospitals, and being an administrator.'

'So you like my mysteries?'

'Oh yeah,' he says, smoothing my hair back from my face.

'Then why are you trying to solve me?'

'You were thirty-eight, working with Petra, and you shed early,' he says, as he holds the glass of water so I can sip through a straw. 'You ran away from London. Why?'

I have no idea how much time has passed. I have been here so long, cocooned, while he tries to form me. This is his script. Everything in life has been revealed as a script, so how can I blame him? It's in the wink of a receptionist underneath a poster that reads *Love is a Warm Layer*; it's in the knowledge that whatever you are will come free in the next layer of loosening skin. Nothing can penetrate me beyond that.

I shake my head.

'We're so close to being together. Properly together. No secrets. Tell me this last thing.' Max's eyes hold tears. 'I know it was terrible. It must have been something terrible.'

'Are you crying for me, or for how bad you feel?'

'Both, Rosie,' he whispers. 'This world. This whole world.'

'No,' I tell him. 'Not your world. These things aren't in

your world. How can you bring them here? How dare you keep me here, and make yourself like them?'

'No, it's for good, Rosie, for good, for you.'

'Max—'

'Listen,' he says. 'Imagine. Imagine a world where love doesn't live in the skin alone. Where it's deep within you, all the time. No skin trade, no incinerators. That world would be a better place, because love could never be bought. Don't you understand that I'm living that dream, right now, and my love comes from that place? That's how you can love me too, if you'll just hold on and take the pills. Remember Paris, walking by the Seine, and I was so nervous when I reached for your hand. But you let me hold it. You let me hold you, and that's when I knew. I loved you beyond my skin.'

'That's not when you loved me. It wasn't when you saw me for the first time, it wasn't in Paris, it wasn't in some moment you've played a thousand times over in your head. It wasn't like that.'

'Then how was it?' He puts his hands on my face, and the skin crackles, like dead leaves against my cheeks. 'Tell me how it was.'

I can't.

I can't play this game any more.

I have no words for it, for this act of recreation. He will make my memories part of his emotional landscape, but they will never be real to him. So I will keep this final part for me alone. I will not dilute it for anyone.

I don't speak. I watch him cry, and I hold it safe, inside. I remember it, just for myself.

The warehouse.

2008. **INSIDE.**

As soon as she opened the unlocked door she knew she wasn't alone.

The air was alive, filled with soft sounds, from a distance: the hum of machinery, and a high whirring she couldn't place.

Rose took a few steps into the partitioned area, stacked cardboard boxes creating a right-angled wall. She caught the occasional voice coming from behind them: women talking, laughing.

She knew she should leave.

The boxes were sealed shut. She took a few quick snaps of them with her phone anyway, and then a couple of close-ups of the stamped marks on the sides that bore an address in London. The contents weren't listed.

Should she rip a hole in one? She took out her penknife – Petra's penknife, in fact, on loan to her – and considered it. But any damage would give away that somebody had been here, and Petra always said:

Don't draw attention to yourself.

If only one of the boxes was open, but the wall was absolute. She felt impotent in the shadow of it.

Petra would say:

Think like an investigator.

She weighed up her options. Damage a box, take a photo. Try to make it look like – what? Rats? Or find the machines making that hum, and photograph them instead.

Rose scanned the makeshift walls. There was a gap, a slim line between two of the boxes in the third row up. She put her eye to it.

The women were talking as they worked. There were maybe thirty of them, operating sewing machines, sitting at tables that had been organised to make three sides of a square. They chatted as their fingers moved independently, accurately, stitching fine white triangles of material into long sheets of patchwork. Light fell in strips from high windows, up above.

Nobody else was visible. Against the far wall of the warehouse was a row of single beds, with crumpled, colourful sleeping bags upon them in different designs: stripes, circles, trucks, trains, butterflies. Another wall of boxes had been built nearby. Rose guessed there were basic cooking and washing facilities behind them. Something told her, in the way the women worked, that this was what they considered to be their home.

Somebody had to be bringing the material, collecting the products, and supplying them with food. But they weren't here at the moment. These women were relaxed, being themselves in their own company. Rose listened carefully. She didn't recognise the language.

She took some photos through the gap, but the focus wouldn't align in the right place. They all looked blurred to her, unclear.

Time to go said Petra's voice, inside her head.

The women were young. Not children, but youthful. As she watched, one of them sat back from her sewing machine and stretched out her arms. Rose noted the curve of her body, and how her belly stood proud from the chair. She was pregnant.

Once her eyes saw it, they recognised it wherever they fell; so many of the women were pregnant. Maybe all of them.

The material they sewed was in such small, delicate pieces. It was skinwork, she thought. Why else hide it away? It had to be skinwork. Rose took her knife and stabbed into one of the boxes, working it into the cardboard until she could reach inside. Her fingers made contact with a soft, giving stretch of sheet. She rubbed it, and felt nothing.

The stitched skin was empty of emotion. There were no memories, no echoes. Instead there was calm. It was good to touch discarded skin and feel nothing upon it; it bore a purity that could have come only from a life that had yet to be touched by love.

It was newborn.

Rose pulled her hand free.

The women – she wanted to tell them, to make them leave, come away. But the door hadn't been locked. And the women were laughing. They had to know what they were sewing, and they were laughing. Touching that fresh clean skin every day, feeling no fear, no worry, no love.

Petra's voice.

She needed it.

It was gone. There was only her own voice, from a place within that she had not known about, telling her to walk away from the women, from the warehouse.

The dual carriageway was in sight, the cars driving past, people on their early morning commutes, so close, and not one of them seeing the warehouse and what was within.

She walked across the scrubland, towards the road. The sun was higher in the sky, burning her wherever it touched. Her skin was alive with it, it wouldn't stay, it couldn't. She took off her black clothes and threw them down, and felt the skin already beginning to peel, to split, but it was not like it had ever been before. She was damaged all the way down, the warehouse had seeped through her; she was soft and pulpy underneath. It was impossible to walk on, the skin was sliding away and she had to be free of it. She fell.

> • <

Hands were upon her, squeezing.

Rose looked at the hands on her own skin, and found she was whole, and new. It shocked her so much that she couldn't speak. She had expected to die.

'I've got you,' Petra said. 'Can you walk?' The squeezing became tugging. 'Get up for me. Get dressed.'

The clothes, collected, rasped against the new skin. She cried as Petra tugged them into place. She never wanted to wear those clothes again.

Then Petra gathered up the old skin and flicked her silver lighter, touching the flame to it. It burned very quickly, down to a fine ash. The smell of smoke was so strong; Rose realised it couldn't be from the skin alone. She turned her head, following the scent. Black smoke. The warehouse. But where were the women?

They made it back to the car and Petra drove. After a time Rose placed their direction; they were going to Wiltshire.

'I can't do this any more,' she said.

'I know,' said Petra.

2013. SNIPS.

Anna Mallory snips away with scissors, starting at my toes. I feel the blade inch up the outside of my knee to my thigh first on one leg, then the other. The skin sticks and has to be peeled back carefully in long strips. Finally that old skin is in pieces.

I concentrate on the sensitive new skin being exposed to the air, already beginning to harden. My stomach, my arms, my shoulders are all released. My face.

'There,' she says.

Max hovers. 'Did it work?'

'It looks good. No damage to the new layer.'

'Right. Great. You can go then.'

She opens her mouth, as if to argue, and then departs, taking Taylor with her, leaving the door ajar.

I won't forget her, or what's she's done here. I won't forget either of them.

As if he can read my thoughts, Max says, 'It worked. Imagine how many people these treatments can help.'

I don't reply.

He goes to the wardrobe and chooses one of the dresses that hangs next to his remaining skins. It's yellow. He brings it out and shows it to me.

'You wore it in Paris,' he says, but it doesn't look familiar.

'Untie me, then.'

Once the restraints are off, I try to stand but my legs are too weak. Max helps me lower the dress over my head.

'I shouldn't put anything harsh on your skin for a while,' he says. 'I want so much to hold you, but I'm afraid it will hurt.'

His tenderness reaches me. 'It's okay. Just be gentle.'

So he sits beside me on the bed and hugs me, and it does hurt. Old emotions on new skin, love and disgust and hatred and all of it together: it's too much for one person to feel. But I want him to have this moment, to remember, to embellish it in his endlessly replaying memory after I go.

'There.' I push him away. 'That's long enough. Will you do something for me, Max?'

'Anything.'

'Stop taking pills. Any pills. Shed that skin. You've been in it too long. It's changed you.'

'But we love each other again.'

I miss the Max who would never have done a thing like this with a ferocity that cements my decision. 'I won't take any more pills. I won't stay.'

'You don't want to stay cured? After all you've told me?'

'You don't know what a cure is,' I say. 'You don't even know what the real illness is, here.'

He clenches his fists, and says, 'I could make you stay.'

But I know this scene, this melodrama of ours, is played out, and he knows it too. 'Don't make it any worse than it needs to be.'

'No.' He sighs. 'Well, it was worth a shot.'

And, with that, he gets up from the bed and turns on all his charm to become a movie star with a hint of Little Boy Lost underneath. 'It was madness, I guess, but it came from a good place. Do you believe that? And it will help millions of sufferers. I just need your word—'

'I won't tell anyone.'

'You're very kind. You know, I think you're right. You're not the girl I fell in love with. My Rosie would have had my balls for a stunt like this.'

Am I the forgiving sort, then, this time around? Can I finally forgive the very worst things? I should have him locked up. I want him locked up. But I'm out of interest in what should or shouldn't happen. 'Stop taking the pills, Max. We're done. I don't want to see you again.'

'It's probably for the best,' he agrees.

'I'm going now.'

'I'll get Taylor to call you a cab.' He shrugs. 'I've been here so long and I find myself calling it a cab. I guess I'm still American, deep down.'

So we go upstairs, and Taylor calls me a cab or a taxi or whatever we want to name it now, while all the time I feel my new skin hardening under the touch of that light summer dress.

'Where do you want to be dropped?' she asks, her tone all business. But she can't look at me. Her hands are shaking. I wonder why she did it. Why she helped him hurt me.

'The train station.'

'No, Max will foot the bill. Take the taxi all the way.'

'What day is it?'

'It's Sunday.'

'Wiltshire, then.'

She nods, and we're done.

2013. **MUSEUM PIECE.**

'It's on the local news,' Petra says, and hands me her phone. There it is: the smoking pile of wreckage that was Mallory Peace Industries in Chichester. Three dead. The story beneath details the breakout of the blaze. Cause unknown.

'Pretty,' I say. I feel no blame. I was somewhere else entirely. A headline catches my eye, and I click on the link.

Black Overdose Stuns Film Community

I check through the article. There are no updates. He's still in intensive care after taking all those pills that caused a massive skin shed, at least three layers gone in twenty-four hours. He isn't expected to live long.

I wondered if he might do something like that, one day. I could almost say he always had it in him.

And yet I miss my Max. I miss him so much; the treatment brought what I loved about him back to me. The Max who is now lying in intensive care, I'm not interested in. He deserves to die.

I hand back the phone. 'Thanks,' I say. 'For your help.'

Paddington is business as usual. We stand under the row of boards and I find the next one to Bristol Temple Meads. Platform eight, ten minutes to go.

'I've cleared it with Phin,' she says. 'He'll deal directly with Taylor. When he finds her.'

Phineas Spice – the man who diagnosed me in his spare time, and whom I would never want to get on the wrong side of. I would pity Taylor if I didn't hate her so much. I can't understand how she could help him. I don't think I'll ever understand it. It's a question that will follow me.

'It was so good to see you,' I say, and it's not a lie. Maybe Aunt Alice is right; maybe friendship, above all things, can be kept, when it's not based on something else. Envy, could we call it? My desire to be her, stronger than my desire to know her, is gone.

'Did you enjoy the museum, this morning?'

I shrugged. 'Actually, the Stuck Six were less impressive than I thought they would be. Those skins felt more like a novelty act than something deep and meaningful. I think perhaps love is overrated.'

'You turning into a cynic?'

'Maybe. Yeah. Yep, I'm a cynic now.'

'Really?'

'Really.'

'So what's a cynic going to do in Bristol?'

'Don't laugh.'

'I won't.'

'I'm going to take a course in interior design,' I tell her.

'Or you could come back and work with me?' Her mouth quirks. 'No, I know, I know, go on then, get on the train.'

'You're so much stronger than me. But that's okay.'

She looks older, for a moment, as she thinks about it. 'No,' she says. 'Not stronger. Just happier to burn it all down. I make the worst things burn so that I feel better. I've only ever been trying to teach you that trick, because we're the same in so many ways. Don't you get it? That's why I gave you a job, and kept you close. We saw the high life, the dream, and left it behind for reality. We're the same.'

'We're not,' I tell her, and we hug. My skin is still a little tender, but I think I can live with it.

PART THREE

Introduced by Mikhael Stuck

Ladies and gentlemen, thanks for that warm welcome, and thanks to the Film Institute for asking me to introduce this screening of the first and last film by the visionary director Max Black: *Sticking Point*.

Max was one of a kind.

He was best known as an actor, and in that he excelled. But since his death nine years ago it has been my goal to make his talent as a director better known to the world, based on the footage he shot whilst attempting to tell the story of my life, and the lives of five others. We became known through the media as the Stuck Six, and everybody thought they knew everything there was to know about us.

But there was so much more.

When people are deeply in love we say they become like one person, one soul, united. I don't think that's true. We retain our individuality, and our right to our own interpretation of the love we share. Max was deeply interested in that idea. Not the notion of getting to the truth at the heart of the Stuck Six, but of realising there was no one truth about us. He bought the rights to Howard's autobiography, but that wasn't what he was filming. He talked to all of us, and he became my friend when I realised he was trying to construct something complex. Something both moving, and fair to my life.

I found a like mind in Max Black.

When I first met him I was surprised at how different he was from his media persona. I thought he would use his charm on me to get what he wanted, but instead he did something that people rarely do. He listened to me. He wanted to understand what having that love, and losing it, had done to me and to my family. We began to talk regularly in preparation for his film, and often the conversation focused on how different the world would be without moulting. He pictured a time when love cannot be bought or sold, lost or gained in a skin.

I wonder what he would have made of the huge changes we have all faced in the last few years as that world has become a reality. I think he would have been overjoyed. I only wish he had waited to see it.

New studies show that over seventy per cent of the UK's population now take a daily supplement of Suscutin, delaying the moulting process indefinitely. We now have the choice whether to moult or to remain in the skin that loves. We can leave love behind when we're ready.

This means that now, in the year 2022, Max's only work as a director is already outdated. He's not alone in this. Every piece of art made before 2020 is a historical record. To watch, read, or listen to anything made before that date can feel like the equivalent of watching a public information film about the horrors of smallpox. These problems no longer apply to us, do they?

I've asked myself many times, particularly once Suscutin

came along, why I've spent so much time working to get *Sticking Point* finished, and to the attention of the general public. Even once I had enlisted the support and belief of our director, Sofie, and the backing of our distributor, Silverfish, I wondered what I was attempting to do. Why does this one film matter so much when there are so many other films, finished films, on the subject of love already? Surely this is the time for new artists and new visions?

I was surprised, when I looked deep inside myself, to realise that the answer wasn't based purely on my personal connection to Max. It sprang from my belief that when someone's way of living becomes history, it doesn't automatically become irrelevant.

Love is still love. It's going to take us all a while to figure that out, maybe. But whether we feel it alone, or with a special person, or in a group, it is the same emotion. Whether it lasts for one skin or one minute, or forever. In its essence, in its time of existence, it is the same, and it unites us all.

I can't think of a film that explores that concept better than *Sticking Point*, and I never knew a person who understood that better than Max Black. Thank you for watching. I hope you enjoy the film.

> • <

After the screening there are drinks to be drunk, congratulations to be borne, photos to be taken with Sofie and the suits. We all smile and wrap our arms around each other's backs. We stare straight ahead as if we share a vision, one way, travelling. Fuck it, fuck them all and their demands and compromises. It's not the film I wanted but

I'm done with it, and with them all. I've done my best by Max, and now maybe I can sleep.

Yes, I can sleep. I sneak out, find a cab, and don't bother to undress once I'm through the door. I fall on the bed, and it all goes away. I've let him down, but I've done my penance. I've got nothing bad left to dream about.

The phone wakes me up early. It's Gwen.

'You should have come last night,' I say, and she says, 'Mik, can you get here? It's back.'

SOMETHING TERRIBLE.

I ask her all the right questions, and try to make sense of her answers. I find myself saying 'Right' after each reply, as if things are being sorted into the correct order.

'You couldn't tell me you were having more tests?' is my final question. The one I have to ask, for my own sake.

Gwen looks terrible. This was a fit woman, tall and strong and capable – a bodyguard, for Christ's sake. All of the qualities I associate with her have been sucked out of her body by this disease. Her skin is the wrong colour and texture. It's too white and papery on her face, dry and cracked, and blotched with red that has coagulated into purple swellings behind her ears, striping down her neck. When did I last see her? Surely she didn't look like this.

'You've lost so much already,' she says. 'I kept hoping it would be—'

'A bad dream? This isn't about me.'

'You're the one who'll get left behind.'

This cottage. This cottage is too small, I should have bought her a bigger one. I can't pace in this living room; I can't breathe with this low-beamed ceiling pressing down on me, the wood painted black, everything about it belonging to some other version of England. I take back what I said last night – screw the past, forget it, it makes no sense. Let's start again.

Although the future's not looking any better.

'Sit down,' she says.

'Let's just stay in the present, okay?' I sit on the sofa, beside her, and feel like a hulking mess next to her new fragility. I shouldn't have driven after the amount I drank last night.

I'm probably still over the limit.

'From the look of you it was a good night,' she says.

'It really wasn't.'

'You want painkillers?'

'Yes.' I rub my temples while she gets up, unfolding with a delicacy that makes me feel ashamed of my mere headache.

'Ibuprofen or one of my personal stash?' she calls from the kitchen.

'You choose.'

She comes back with a glass of water and two white oblong pills. I knock them back. 'So how long?'

'I thought you wanted to stay in the present.'

'I'm asking how long we can stay in the present for.'

'Not long,' she says, curling back up to her original position, knees tucked in, spine curved against the cushions. Why should she say that so calmly? I want her to rage with me, to challenge it all. We had plans for after I'd done with the film. We were going to go travelling and do things, physical things like climbing and swimming and hiking. It all had a reality to me that is growing more ephemeral by the minute, and I can't grasp it, or her.

Gwen doesn't do television, so the sofa is directly in front of the bay window, looking out over the unkempt garden. The iron gate at the end of the path is ajar – I must have forgotten to shut it properly – and beyond it, on the main road through the village, I can see my BMW and the pub opposite. It's one of those ones with low, dark windows and dirty white walls. It's called The Lamb.

'I hate Devon,' I say. 'I should have talked you out of living here. Come back to London with me. I'll find a better doctor.'

She shakes her head.

'I'll sell this place from under you if you piss me off. I'm serious this time, Taylor. Move your arse to London and get checked over properly.'

She doesn't say anything for a while. Then, out of the blue, 'Studies show a huge increase in Epidermal Sclerosis in the past five years. I heard rumours that they're looking at Suscutin as a possible cause.'

'Stop reading tabloids. You've spent too long sitting down here, looking out of the window and waiting for shit to happen.'

'Come on!' There it is: the fire, the heart of her. 'Mik, it's the pills, it's the pills, it's only what I deserve.'

'Nobody deserves this. And if it's the pills, they'll prove a link.'

'And do what? A few adverse reactions against a multi-million pound industry? It won't change anybody's mind. It hasn't changed your mind. You're still taking your daily dose, aren't you?'

'You know I am. There's no proof, Gwen.'

She nods, and slumps back down. 'I get it. It's much better that we're all free to love each other forever. If we can find anyone to love us back.'

She's so bitter. But she knows who I am; she knows the deal. I don't do love, not now, not ever again. 'Listen, you're my best friend, but I—'

She punches my arm. Once, not too long ago, it would have hurt. 'Shut up, you moron. You're so self obsessed.'

'Fuck you!'

She laughs, then says, 'Sell the damned cottage. Just pay my hospice bills instead. There's a nice one with a duck pond just outside Exeter.'

'Seriously? You're going to meekly accept your impending death because there's a duck pond to sit by?'

'It's not treatable, Mik. It's gone beyond the first layer. It's all the way through me, now. I smell it. I want to be in a place where we all smell as bad as each other.'

'I think you'll find that smell is my hangover.'

'Go wash then, you pig.'

> • <

When I come back downstairs, only ten minutes later, it's all different. Death is accepted, done and dusted, sitting down to breakfast with us. How can that happen? She's made toast and coffee in her magazine-standard kitchen, and she's all business.

'Listen,' she says, as I butter the toast and layer on marmalade, 'there's something you need to do for me.'

'Fire away.'

'You need to find someone. Someone that I have to apologise to.'

'Making amends time already?'

'No,' says Gwen. 'Don't. Don't make a joke about it.'

'Is this to do with the day that you left Max?' I ask. The day we never talk about.

She doesn't answer me, exactly. 'I don't want to die without having said sorry. You can understand that, can't you?'

She knows I can.

She knows how important apologies have been to me, and how hard I have worked for them: to get them, and to give them. Finishing Max's film has been one long apology to him, even though he can never accept it.

'It's not only that.' Her fingers pluck at the collar of her white shirt – why does she still dress like a professional even though she's been out of work for years? It's like she's never let her guard down; she's still looking for threats.

'Then what?'

'Do you remember when you first helped me out? What you said to me?'

'I said, whatever you need.'

'Not that bit. I told you I had to disappear, get far away from there, and you said: Okay. And you said: Nothing is unforgivable, though.'

'That's right.'

'You still believe that?'

'I do.' I have to.

'Then find Rose Allington for me,' she says, and she hasn't looked so desperate since she turned up outside my caravan one morning on Max's Sussex estate, halfway through filming, and begged me to take her away, hide her from herself.

'Just tell me,' I say, on an impulse. 'This one time. It was so long ago. Tell me what you did, and what Max did, and be done with it.'

She rolls her eyes. 'One more time, Mik. It's not about you.'

'Oh that's right, I forgot for one second. Lucky you were here to remind me. So where do I look for this Rose Allington? I've always wanted to play detective.'

'You start by finding someone I used to know. He's called Phineas Spice.'

JUST A TRIM.

It occurred to me to go back to my original name, of course. After we became press fodder, and being a Stuck was literally that – being mired in that role as one of the six happiest people on Earth, just waiting for it to end. Of course it had to end. We all knew that. The six of us, the reporters, the people who were searching the internet every day for updates. And it did end.

I always intended to go back to my old name. Mikhael Gusin. But when it came to it, I couldn't. I wasn't that person any more. I couldn't find a new name that suited me either. What do people do, sit down and make one up? Is there a list, somewhere, to pick from by your particular trauma?

No, I'm Mikhael Stuck. It fits. We all took Howard's surname at first because we wanted to be stuck together, and now it describes who I am with an ironic precision that continues to entertain me.

Not so for Phineas Spice, who has gone back to his birth name of Alexander Joseph Murray.

It didn't take long to find him. In fact, I didn't find him at all. I paid someone to do that. I don't think Gwen really had in mind that I would need to get dressed up in a trenchcoat or a deerstalker, and do the legwork. I hired an agency, and they tracked him down in a couple of days. A courier dropped off a thick file to my flat in Kensington, and I read all about nightclubs and skin fights, gambling and prostitution. And Starguard, of course.

I know exactly what kind of person is cutting my hair right now.

The shop is empty. I waited outside in the car, trying to

get Phineas alone. Alexander, I should say. He's a short man in a loud shirt, the collar open, a gold chain hanging loose. He's bald himself, and shiny under the recessed spotlights of his black and chrome decor. He trims away at my locks with expert fingers; you'd think he's been doing this all his life.

'Not too much off the top, thanks.'

'No problem.'

'How did you choose the name?' I ask him.

He blinks; I watch him in the large rectangular mirror before us, a slant of the summer sunshine falling across his chest, but he's perfectly calm as he says, 'Pardon?'

The sharp snaps of the scissor blades are loud in my ear. 'The name of your shop. Nicky's. Are you Nicky?'

'That was my dad. He owned it. After he died I took over.'

'I'm sorry. When was that?'

'2018? Yeah.'

'You weren't a hairdresser before then?'

He stops cutting, and straightens up. 'I trained as a barber, years ago, out of school. Came back to it late.'

'Wow.'

The brush is applied to the back of my neck, sweeping away loose strands to the linoleum floor. 'You're done,' he says.

'Thanks.'

This is a quiet town, barely map-worthy in the depths of Bedfordshire. Shefford has a small supermarket and one cafe, from what I can see. The barber shop actually has competition; there's another one, three doors down. Why do hairdressers flock together? One turns up on a street and chances are there'll be two more on the same stretch in no time at all.

Give me a city any day. Give me anything but little communities with their big mouths. The locals were smiley and pleasant, but keen enough to give the papers a scoop, back when the six of us lived in Cambridgeshire. Not far from here, actually.

I should have come here with a question in mind, or a way into the conversation I want to have. Instead, I end up standing at the reception desk, credit card in hand once the transaction has been completed, hesitating. I must look like an idiot.

This man was scary, once. He had things done to people. He was in charge.

He points a finger at me. 'You're Mickey Stuck, aren't you?'

'Yeah.'

'I thought I recognised you.' He doesn't say more.

It's now or never. 'Actually, we have a mutual friend.'

'Is that so?'

'Gwen Taylor. She used to work for you. Starguard.'

'So she did.' He reappraises me, straightens up. Hardens. 'It was a long time ago since she disappeared off. Still, water under the bridge. Max Black, that's the link, right? I haven't thought about him in years. You met her through Max?'

'That's right.'

'So how is she doing? Is she finally going to pay me back what she owes me? All that bodyguard training, setting her up in a job, it wasn't cheap.'

'I'll pay you back. Whatever, name it.' I shouldn't react, I know; he's just trying to get a rise out of me. Play who's got the biggest wad.

'Just the eight quid for the trim was enough from you, thanks. We're done.'

Now he's got my back up. 'Did you get your pound of flesh from most of your girls one way or another, then?'

His eyes snap to mine. 'I had a business, they were employees. That was it.'

'So was Rose Allington one of your employees?'

He walks past me to the door, turns the top lock, and lowers the venetian blind with a swish. How come that action makes the shop feel so much smaller?

He leans back against the door. 'How old are you?'

'Why do you want to know?'

'Because right now you look really young. Really young. So what is it? Taylor wants to track down Rose? She wants to finish what she started?'

'She's dying. Skin disease. She wants to see Rose. That's all I know.'

'And you said you'd find her?'

'I promised.' Surely even somebody who was once Phineas Spice can understand that.

He smiles at me. 'Really young,' he says. 'Come on, come in the back, I'll put the kettle on.'

He's not threatening at all, here, in this small back room; in fact, he's welcoming to me amidst the shelves of shampoo, conditioner and dye. There's a plastic chair and I sit, my leg pressed up against a trolley, the top tray of which contains so many pink plastic clips, while he makes tea. The smell of wet hair, dried hair, is strong. I suppose you get used to it.

'That's really disappointing,' he says, when he asks how easy he was to track down. 'But I only went back to my roots, really, didn't I? Roots. I wouldn't mind some of those again.' He touches his bald head, runs a hand down its slick curve, then hands me a mug of tea. 'I used to shave it to look hard, down in London. Get taken seriously. Then I stopped, moved back here, and it wouldn't grow back. Look at you, you've got no worries yet, have you? Does baldness run in your family? My dad was bald at thirty.'

I think of my father's thick hair, still curling around his ears and temples – or it was when I last saw him, a year or so ago. 'No.'

He nods. 'You're really going to go through with this? For Taylor's sake?'

'She needs my help.' One of the few things about me that I like is the fact that I always help Gwen when she needs it.

'Sounds like she got lucky when she met you.'

'We're not together,' I tell him, although I'm not sure why.

He digests this information. 'What was it like? Being with five people at the same time?'

Does he mean love or sex? It's not one of those uncomfortable male moments, jokey yet sweaty, that I'm not keen on. I've had those before, after a few drinks, where men get drunk enough to ask me what went where or if I was a giver or a taker, all that crap. I answer as if love is all there is. 'Confusing, but good. Happy, for a while.'

'Sounds like all love stories. You were, what? Nineteen, twenty, when it happened to you? You were the youngest, the last to join, right? The good looking one.'

'You seem to know a lot about it already,' I tell him.

'I read the book. The oldest one wrote it. Howard, was it?'

'Well, see the film. It's in cinemas now.'

'Max Black's film.'

'Yeah.'

'No,' says Alexander, or Phineas, or whatever. 'I won't be going to see that. I don't want his thoughts in my head.'

'What do you mean?'

'I've seen and heard about a lot of shit, but I don't want to own the oil paintings.'

'I don't understand. You knew him? You didn't like him?'

'Wow,' he says. 'Listen, forget all about this stuff. Forget about Taylor. Go your own way.'

'I'm looking for Rose Allington. Gwen wants to apologise to her while she still can. That's it. That's all I know. I don't care what you think you know, or what it matters. I'm just doing a friend a favour.'

He wets his lips with his tongue, then puts his own mug down in the small sink, beneath a wall-mounted boiler that looks older than I am. He's a snake; I read his file, I know what he is. He makes money from other people's suffering. He's playing me, there's some angle in this, there has to be. But he's squeezing past my knees, past the tray with the pink clips. He leaves the room, and I still have no idea what he wants from me.

I sit there for a while before I feel certain he's not coming back.

Eventually I put my mug down next to his, quietly, and walk back into the main part of the shop.

He's at the door, hand on the top lock, looking out over the lazy travels of those on the main street. The afternoon sun has moved round to bathe half the room in its light; I have to squint when he swivels around, to see his expression. But I can't guess how he's feeling.

'You get started on a path,' he says. 'You never start down

it yourself. It's only later you realise – that was the person who pushed me down it. Later, if you're lucky, someone else – a better person – sets you on a better road. One that leads to a good place.'

'That's what you're trying to do for me, is it? Is that what you did in London? In your nightclub? With all the employees of Starguard?'

'It's what I've always tried to do.'

'So who set you on the wrong path, then?'

'That doesn't concern you,' he says, and I glimpse the man in the file. 'I don't know where Rose is. She fell off my radar not long after Max died. If you're serious about finding her, you should go look for Petra Cross.'

It's a name that's not unfamiliar to me. I wonder if Gwen has mentioned her before. 'Where can I find her?'

'Doesn't mean a thing to you, then?' He smiles, but I get the feeling he doesn't find it as funny as he's pretending.

'Just tell me.' Why am I always having to say that to people?

'Don't judge us all too hastily when you get your answers, okay?' He opens the door, and swings it back. 'It was a long time ago. Before Suscutin, which I'm guessing you take. I'm not judging you. I take it too.'

'Most people do.'

'Yes,' he agrees. 'Most people do. Some don't like themselves for it.'

'Like you, you mean? Why not?'

He hesitates, then says, 'I like the dream it's selling us. Just not the fact it has to be sold.'

'What dream is it selling?'

'That love lasts forever.'

Ah, now I understand. He's fallen in love and moved up here for the quiet life, sustained by Suscutin, but he misses London. He misses being Phineas Spice. 'So where's your other half?' I ask him. 'Your dream?'

'Wrong way round,' he says, amused at me. 'I made the changes so that if love comes along, I'll be ready for it. Worthy of it.' He winks. 'One of these days, it'll find me.'

'In Shefford, Bedfordshire?'

'You are just so young, aren't you, mate?' he says. 'Right. Out you go. Don't come here again.'

RENOVATIONS.

If twenty-nine is so young, why do I feel so crumpled? Time has folded me this way and that, and left its marks.

Twenty-nine is old enough to have seen things change, and to change along with them. It's more than old enough to know things might change back, one day. But not yet. There's no point in racing towards it. There's no reason to force change in the hope someone likes it.

I'm not like Phineas/Alexander, who's sitting in his shop pretending he's become lovable, and that some good man or woman will notice. I'm not stupid enough to imagine that could work.

I can't reconcile that dreamer with the man I read about in the file. If there's one question I wish I'd asked him, it would be why did you choose such a stupid pseudonym? Phineas Spice is a pathetic name.

But even if I knew why he called himself that, I get the feeling I'll never understand him. The file, the facts: they give me no insight into a person. It's the equivalent of somebody reading press cuttings about me and thinking they'd know what happened when I was part of the Six. You can't get to know someone through the written word. A compilation of actions, laid bare on the page, have all motivation missing from the information.

I find myself driving east.

> • <

Living on the edge of Grafham Water seemed like a good idea, once we came to the attention of the press. They couldn't get at us from every side; that long calm lake – a reservoir, in fact – deterred just about all of them, except for the few who were desperate enough to hire boats from the local sailing club, from time to time.

I stop the car down the road from what used to be our house, on the verge where the paparazzi used to park. I get out, and stretch away the hours of driving. It's a warm evening, and still. I skirt around, keeping a distance from the barn conversion, large, on a remote part of the water. There are no cars parked directly outside. We rented it, paying for six months up front after we'd been brought to the attention of the world as the Stuck Six. Howard made the decision to give an exclusive interview to get the money together. He didn't consult us. But I was grateful that he organised everything, and didn't make me speak in public.

I was different, then.

He was in charge, and when he said it was time to leave Birmingham, our jobs, our studies, our friends, we did it. Some articles called him a cult leader, but the truth is that somebody had to be the boss of us. The entity we were. You don't get six people together for any period of time and find decision-making works in a democratic sense. For one thing, there's not an odd number to sway a vote.

The hawthorn provides cover from the big window at the front, and I skulk around to the side of the house, where changes start to become obvious to me. There's a storage area with a slanted roof jutting out from the wall, between the kitchen and the bathroom windows. Logs are arranged, pyramid-style, inside – a good supply. A burner must have been installed, ready for a cold winter.

But that was always Dan, stocked up for the worst situation while hoping for the best. He was so adamant we would make it through the difficult times, stay together even after he moulted. But when I said I couldn't stand it any more he was the one who gave me the money he'd been saving, and an address of an old friend in London who I could stay with.

I wonder why he chose to buy this place when the money came through, and to live here still.

I should knock at the front door, like a guest, in case he's in. But I end up at the back door, trying the handle as if I still have the right to enter.

It's locked.

My instinct tells me nobody's home.

I look through the glass pane and see little differences everywhere rather than the things that have stayed the same. These variations on my past jump into clarity: an amateur's painting of Grafham Water at sunset with a charm about it; a silver spice rack; an open cookbook and a blue striped teapot. None of these objects look like Dan's taste to me, and everything is far too tidy. He's living here with someone, is my guess, and he hasn't told me. Or any of the others. I think if he chose to tell one of us, it would be me. We told each other everything.

But perhaps lovers always say that of each other, and it's never exactly true.

I hope he's happy. And other clichés.

I move away from the door.

We never swam in the Water; I don't know why that's so strongly in my mind. We didn't even spend long looking at it. It would have been a photo opportunity extraordinaire for the photographers that camped outside, or sailed past.

Mickey Stuck, looking depressed and alone – is there trouble in paradise? And to strip down, reveal my body to them, was unthinkable. Mickey Stuck, youngest member of the Six, showing off the physique that makes him so desirable.

I take a stroll down the footpath, overgrown, that leads to the familiar view that trapped me while the world waited for us to end. There, at least, nothing has changed. Nothing apart from me.

Gwen is dying, and I'm looking at an old view.

I take off everything, shed my clothes on the grass and wade into the water. It swallows me, claims me. Fuck, it's cold, my lungs tighten with it, but as it slides up over my skin my body adjusts, and then I'm swimming. If there was someone with me, waiting on the shore for me, I would call – Come in, the water's fine.

It is fine. It's good, and it's only for me. I don't need to share it. If I wanted to, I could swim right across this reservoir. I'm fit, I'm still young, I'm free.

Of course, I'd be naked at the other end.

So I splash around for a bit longer in the late afternoon light, trying out one stroke, then another; I even do a bit of butterfly, feeling my shoulders working hard, starting up a deep ache in the muscles. When I realise I'm shivering I head back to the shore.

There's a flash of red on the footpath. It swings, and emerges from the bushes; it's a handbag, suspended on a woman's shoulder, giving away her presence like a bright target. She has something in her hands.

She holds the small object up and out, in front of her. I watch her gesture, and place its meaning. She's taking photos of me on her phone.

'Come on then,' I shout, and then I'm walking towards her, naked, shouting loud and fast, and she turns and skitters away behind the bushes, out of my view in seconds.

Common sense kicks in.

I stop chasing her. I return to the water's edge and put on my clothes, having to struggle with them as they stick to my wet skin.

Fuck it, fuck her, fuck it all.

> • <

I should probably phone the others. Howard, at least; I should tell him what's happened. I'm guessing it'll take a while for the woman to agree a price with a newspaper or website, and then the story will appear. That gives me a window of maybe a day. I should attempt some damage limitation, as least by explaining to Dan what I was doing outside his house, naked, swimming in the reservoir.

As soon as I work it out myself, I'll let him know.

For now, London is what I need. It's past ten when I get in, and the tiled hall with its clean mirrors placed along the white walls is just what I need. I take the stairs to my top-floor flat, and am relieved to find it's still not a home to me. It's just a space I rest in sometimes, where I don't have to be recognisably anything. Not even a person, really.

I've lived here for a few months. One of the things I like best about it is that my cleaner keeps moving everything. I like the thought of her, shifting it all about, rearranging to her satisfaction while pretending it's for mine. She works for an agency; I don't even know her name. Whenever I get a glimpse of her, early in the morning, she puts a finger to her lips and tiptoes off to another room.

Perhaps that's the kind of relationship Max liked, with his female bodyguards. They took care of him without once expecting a word from him. Maybe I should get a guard too. But no, I don't want that kind of life any more. Having a bodyguard is a bit like proclaiming you're worthy of one, and trouble invites trouble. I don't want to be the focus of any more fantasy or jealousy.

I never should have swum in the water. Stupid, stupid.

I eventually find the instant coffee at the back of a cupboard, and make myself a cup, enjoying the way the smell awakens the flat.

There's always something to apologise for. I've done something terrible, Gwen said, the day we left Max behind. The day he took all those pills. These sins, I can't believe in them. And Alexander, Phineas, whatever he called himself – he made out like Max was some sort of monster. But these people are my friends. These are the people who found me at my lowest, and saved me. These crimes feel like a child's crimes; I am finally a parent, with transgressions brought before me, and I must smile and mend the toy, and say *All better now*. Is that my role here?

But Max is dead and Taylor is dying, and there are so many pieces to glue together.

The sleek wall-mounted television, background company, reports a large anti-Suscutin rally at Westminster. In the aerial views the streets are packed, and then the camera cuts to the inevitable close-up of angry faces, and a car on fire. Not here in Kensington of course, but somewhere not far away people are raging, screaming, fighting to restore what they think of as the natural way of things. But they are a minority.

The camera cuts back to the main desk, and the serious presenter moves on to similar rallies being held across European capitals today, and protest gatherings across the US. She doesn't mention Africa or Asia, and she doesn't mention a possible link to Epidermal Sclerosis. It's as if these things belong in different programmes, or not in the news at all.

How am I meant to know things if nobody will tell me the truth?

Flicking through the channels, I land upon Max's face, young and handsome, playing a cop tracking down a serial killer who makes girls fall in love with him so he can slice off their skin and wear it. All of his expressions, his movements, are familiar to me, but in a different context. When he's disgusted by the barbarity of a crime, I see it as that time he hated the amount of mayonnaise I put in his sandwich. When he expresses his love for his beautiful young wife, who will undoubtedly end up in danger, I see him on our ridiculous camping trip, in his own backyard of his Sussex Downs estate, telling me that it's a great sunset and a wonderful world, and he could do with another beer.

Yeah, that was a great camping trip, even if we didn't go further than a mile from his house and the tent leaked.

While he tracks down the killer I tap the name Petra Cross into my phone.

Two things:

She has her own Wikipedia page.

She's dead.

I scroll down the page, and the reason why I know her name comes back to me. Every person at the Suscutin march, out there rioting on the streets tonight, would have told me in a heartbeat that she is their hero, their martyr. She attempted to burn down the biggest Suscutin laboratory in the UK three years ago, and didn't escape the blaze she had started. Firefighters managed to save the building, but her body was found within; she'd climbed into a janitor's cupboard when she was unable to escape, and died of smoke inhalation.

There are lots of memorial sites and mentions of her name, but I find only a few pictures of her online; in this day and age it's quite an achievement to have been so camera-shy. There's a photo of her with a military unit, in camouflage gear. They are arranged in two rows, and she is front left, kneeling, with dark smears on her face and twigs sticking up from her helmet. She looks very young.

There's also a photo of her after she died, curled up in that small cupboard; someone took a picture of her, and slapped it up on websites and wherever, at a price. Her face is half-twisted away, and her limbs are folded up tight.

I wish there was a third photo of her, smiling naturally at the camera, or maybe caught unawares with a group of friends, looking the wrong way or pulling a funny face. Then she would become someone I might recognise if I passed her on the street.

There's nothing to suggest a link to help me find Rose Allington, but there is one interesting aspect. Both Petra and Gwen are ex-military; could Rose be the same? Starguard: that's the link. You're a superstar and you want a cool bodyguard, then you employ an ex-military looker. Max always used Starguard.

Wherever I look, Max's face pops up. Right now, he's saving the day as his beautiful wife gets kidnapped by the serial killer. He finds her in time, punches the killer in the face, and seals the whole deal with a long, loving kiss. Wife, and skins, saved.

I'm not going to pass this puzzle back to the private investigators I hired before. I'm going to solve it myself. I want to understand it in ways that a report can't tell me.

I start working through all the Google results for Petra Cross, methodically, while the serious news presenter returns and runs through the same lines about the rally all over again.

> • <

'What happened?' says Howard. 'Your film not doing well enough at the box office, so you have to strip off for the publicity?'

'Don't be a dick,' I tell him. 'Have you spoken to Dan about it?'

'He says you should have let yourself in and grabbed a towel. Apparently the spare key is still under that pot Sunetra made at night school.'

'Seriously?' I had forgotten all about that pot, and her experiment at integrating into the local community while learning a brand new life skill. It lasted about four weeks, as all her projects did, before she hit on poetry, and her one creation – a lopsided pot with a thick handle and a patchy green glaze – got consigned to the garden as a planter into which nobody planted anything. Not one of us was much of a gardener. 'Tell him I'm sorry.'

'You tell him.'

'I'm busy. I'm doing something for a friend.'

'Are you driving?' he asks.

'I'm on hands free, and keeping my eyes on the road, Howard.'

'Come out to Cologne. You'll love it. Nobody in Germany gives a crap about your skinny-dipping.'

'I said I'm busy.' I pull into the fast lane, and speed up, until I'm going faster than he would like. It's petulant, but it makes me feel better. I shouldn't have accepted his call, but the guilt got to me for a moment.

'The UK can't be the nicest place to be with that headline.'

'At least I didn't make the front page. Somebody got killed in the riots yesterday. I'm page three.'

'How apt,' he says. He always did have that sort of sense of humour. 'Seriously, I'm worried about you. Come and stay for a bit. I'm out all day working, so you won't see that much of me. You're not doing anything, are you? Your film's done.'

'It's not my film. It's Max's film.' I indicate, slow down, and pull into the inside lane. The exit for Swindon is coming up fast.

'Yes, bloody Max,' he says. He was so jealous of my friendship with Max; Max's death didn't seem to change Howard's dislike of him. 'Do you hear yourself? Why do you make out you're still a teenager and I'm your dad? I'm not trying to make you do something you don't want to do, but you seem to go out of your way to piss me off. And you make me feel really old in the process.'

Now he's annoyed, I feel better. A switch flips in my head, and I can relax. 'You are really old,' I tell him.

'I'm thirty-seven and you forgot my birthday. Again. It was last Thursday.'

'Sorry. Many happy returns.'

'You idiot,' he says, but I can hear his smile. 'If you want you could talk to Nicky. She's in London at a convention. Get together, do drinks, or something. Distract her from her serious academic life.'

'I will, but I'm not in London right now, okay? I'll phone her when I get back and she can bore me for hours about romantic fiction in the 1800s or whatever.'

'Okay, cool. It's probably a good idea to be out of London for the time being.' There's a pause. I swear I can hear him thinking. 'Maybe you should give me an address for where you'll be staying, just in case, because I'm going to get our solicitors and media team to just look over—'

I make crackling noises at the back of my throat. 'Sorry Howard... going through... a tunnel...'

'Mik, phones don't even do that any more. You've seen too many old films. Just hang up like a normal person.'

'Can't... hear... you...'

I end the call, and smile to myself all the way to Lyneham.

UNDERNEATH.

The people living in Petra's old house know nothing about its connection to her. They are a quiet couple, living and growing together in a way that probably makes them look older than they are, and they have likeable, open faces as I stand on their doorstep and question them on this hot Saturday afternoon.

The house is one of a row that overlooks the long fence that runs around the laboratories. An RAF base once, my online searching informed me that it was bought at a rock-bottom price by Suscutin six years ago, and revamped for:

The Next Stage of Our Evolution

That was what their website claimed, anyway.

'All the houses around here are owned by employees, now,' says the man. 'It's convenient, that's the main reason we bought. Plus the company has a private security force that does the rounds out on the estate sometimes as well as inside the wire, which is good. They drive round twice a night.'

'Why? Is there trouble?'

'No, it's just because of the protestors, particularly this time of year,' says the woman. 'Petra Cross really used to live here? We bought it at auction. No wonder she tried to burn the laboratories down, if they moved in just next door to her and she hated them so much.'

'She could have moved,' the man points out.

'Why is it so bad at this time of year? With the protestors?' I ask.

'Usually they keep to camping along the back fence, although the farmer keeps trying to get them moved off, and they aren't much bother,' says the woman. It sounds like a very British form of resistance, with an annoyed farmer, camping and everybody determined to make their point without inconveniencing each other any more than necessary. 'But a lot more turn up come the anniversary of the arson attempt, and they stay in the village. They can get a bit loud in the pub, and mess up the churchyard. Excuse me for asking, but aren't you Mickey Stuck?'

So that explains why they're being so loquacious, so helpful. They feel they already know me in some way. There are strange benefits to fame that pop up in the most unexpected of places.

'I am, yeah. It's been lovely to meet you, and thanks for your help.'

'Are you okay?' says the man. 'Do you need to come in and call someone?'

They must have seen the paper; it laid it on thick about the state of my mental health. Or perhaps they think celebrities shouldn't be out, wandering around, unsupervised. Their concern touches me.

'I'm really fine. I'm researching a new film.'

'That's right, you're producing them now, aren't you? That's brilliant,' enthuses the woman, and I'm glad I've ticked all their boxes and given them a good story to tell their friends.

'I only wish…' the man says, hesitant, then presses on, 'that it had been around for you guys. The Six. Suscutin.'

'It was so sad when you broke up,' says the woman.

'It was. Have you two been together long?'

'Eight years,' she says. 'Still going strong. Still in love.' She glances under her lashes at him, a little unsure to speak for him in such a way perhaps, and he takes her hand and squeezes it. They are adorable. What a gift they have – ongoing love, with no expiration date. It's impossible to understand why people want to shut down the laboratories, destroy the drugs, when it can offer this.

Then I think of Gwen: her papery skin, her pain.

'That's amazing,' I say. 'Thanks, guys.'

'You're sure you don't need anything else?'

I shake my head. 'Do you mind if I leave my car parked here for a bit? I'd like to walk into the village and take a look around.'

They are delighted to be of further help. They give me extensive directions, tilting their heads in time as they talk of the path to take.

> • <

It's a short walk, and the fence runs along the length of the path for most of the way. Just before I reach a minimarket, the first shop of the village from this direction, the fence takes a ninety-degree turn and heads off across the Wiltshire fields. I can see a sparse strip of weed-ridden land in the distance that must have been a runway. The main laboratory buildings are hidden from view. There are a few warehouses I can see, but it's impossible to tell if they are from the RAF days or are a new addition.

I carry on past the minimarket, and reach a crossroads that I suspect is the closest thing the village has to a centre. There's a bus stop, a pub, a Chinese takeaway. One of those little shops from which the faintest whiff of incense leaks, with dream catchers and tie-dyed dresses in the window. There are wind chimes hanging outside it, and they make no tinkling noise in this hot, dry afternoon: nothing stirs.

So much for hordes of protestors, getting loud in the pub and destroying the churchyard.

The act strikes me as incongruous – why would they choose the churchyard as their target? I see the short square belfry in the distance, on my left, and walk in its direction. It's a pleasant stroll to St Michael's sturdy walls. Sinking into the grass around it, at skewed angles, are old gravestones with lichen filling their grooves, making most of the names unreadable. I see no signs of obvious disturbance or vandalism as I take my time, weaving amid the stones. Why are the dead so restful? Soon Gwen will be dead, and quietened, serene, against her will. She was never meant to be such things.

When she goes, perhaps my guilty conscience will die too. The result will be something neither of us deserve: peace.

Around the back of the church are the new graves, black granite and white marble in the main, standing straighter because time has not marked them yet. These graves bear flowers: some fresh, some wilted, some no more than sticks in the dirt. One bears so many flowers that they overflow on to the grass and make a fat tail that snakes off to the treeline. The name upon the grey, veined marble stone is Petra. Petra Cross.

So here she is, not cremated, left unburned, which is fitting. And here are her tributes. No wonder they come here and mess up the graveyard with their flowers. She's still in the shade of Suscutin, and that must help to keep their hatred alive.

The dates on the stone remind me there are only two days until the anniversary of her death. People gather on such anniversaries. Old friends come to pay their respects.

I walk back to the pub and inquire after a room.

'All booked up, sorry,' says the man behind the bar, barely glancing at me. He's taken me for a Petra disciple, I think. He hasn't recognised me. It actually occurs to me to say, Do you know who I am? But thankfully that ridiculous instinct passes.

I could find a bigger hotel and run the risk of becoming an object of interest to the staff, the other visitors, and maybe the newspapers if I'm unlucky.

Howard would kill me.

I know what he would want me to do, and – this is a first – I think maybe I want to do it too.

I phone Liz.

> • <

Liz is always the least recognised of us. There's something about her short brown hair and dark eyes, the five feet four of her, which blends into a crowd and renders her invisible. Her ability to stand in a queue and not get served for hours at a time was an ongoing joke with us all. She never received much fan mail, either. Elizabeth Stuck – the only celebrity who nobody knew about.

It made me love her more. I told her once she should take to crime; she would never have been suspected, let alone caught. But of course she didn't. When we all broke up she went back to her maiden name of Jones and became a team manager for one of the huge insurance companies that made their home in the centre of Swindon. The ongoing, faceless business of rules and targets seemed to be made for her.

Upon my arrival at her Swindon flat I sit down in a squashy armchair and she sits opposite, her hands in her lap.

'Thanks,' I say.

'No problem.'

Being in the room with her is difficult. Not painful, but a little sore, and tender, like a new growth of skin over an old wound. We never did say goodbye to each other.

She asks me how long I want to stay.

'Just a couple of days. Is that okay?'

'Of course. Howard said he was worried about you.'

'You speak to him a lot?'

'About once a week. Just to touch base. He phoned me last night.'

Of course, he would phone Liz. The two of them were the oldest, and the most responsible. Her calmness penetrated us all to some degree, and I saw Howard drawing strength from her support, particularly at the end. It wasn't a disguise on her part; she really was that chilled about it all. How, I don't know.

'It's only because of these bloody pictures,' I say, sinking further down into her squashy armchair. Everything in this small living room is either cream-coloured or a deep plum hue, and it's so warm and airless in here, with the windows all sealed up tight. I could fall asleep in a moment.

'The nude ones? He told me about them.'

'You didn't see them?'

'I don't do news,' she says. 'Besides, I've seen it all before.'

Her life is suddenly clear to me. It's a hibernation. Its warm soft stasis appeals at this moment, but it already contains a seed of repulsion that could easily germinate if I stayed here too long. It's so peaceful. But it's not living, not as I would want to live.

'Good thinking,' I say. 'It's all crap, anyway, all this mental health stuff.'

'It's really lovely to see you, Mik. It's not just small talk, I promise, I know how you hate that. Seeing you reminds me that I didn't make it all up. Sometimes the past feels like it didn't happen to me, do you know what I mean? Forgive me, but I didn't go and see the film you've been working on. It could only have made it seem more like someone else's dream.'

This sudden flow of words sounds rehearsed to me; if so, I'm glad I gave her the chance to say them in person.

'That is so very okay, Liz. Everything you've done has always been okay with me.'

How very formal this intimacy is, with timings and sentiments, like the steps of a waltz. All the things I loved about her are here, in the room with us. They are watching us carry out this dance.

'I think,' she says, leaning forward in her own armchair as the octagonal clock on the wall ticks, 'that out of the six of us, we two did each other the least damage in the process of disengagement.'

We never did argue, that's true. We stepped around each other, and took sides in the others' arguments. 'Perhaps that's because we didn't want to hurt each other.'

She shakes her head, and settles her clear gaze upon me. 'It's because we loved each other the least.'

The certainty of her statement is unbearable. She has ranked our love and placed it bottom of the pile. I never once did such a terrible thing. It's a sudden act of violence.

'If that's true for you,' I say, with such delicacy, 'it wasn't the case for me.'

For I loved her deeply, as I did all of us. She wasn't who I went to for talking, true. It was the physicality we created between us that obsessed me, that made me curl up in her bed with her most nights, towards the end. When we made love she grew in stature and significance; she had a vocal tenderness that surrounded me, ensconced me. I let go of everything but her voice, coaxing me inside her. Soft, even waves of sound.

And she loved me less.

'I mean—' She gestures, her fingers splayed, towards me, away from me. 'We were less connected, somehow. Didn't you feel that?'

It's overwhelming: the room, the sinking armchair, this lethargy. I have no strength left to pull myself up, to hide this hurt she's causing. I can feel it on my face, visible to her.

'Don't cry, don't cry,' she pleads, and she gets up, comes to me, drapes herself over me. She sits on my lap and pulls my head against her chest, commanding the situation, yet moving just softly enough that I don't resist. She says, hoarse and low, 'I loved having you in me, I loved you, I loved you, Mik, but it was a love I could let go of. It's not a bad thing that you didn't break my heart, don't you know that? It's a good thing. It means I think of you most fondly, now. I care for you more now.'

She has weighed and measured me, and now I let her comfort me for the shortcomings she has created.

> • <

It's the only time we hug during my visit. Even when we say goodbye, and tell each other how good it was to spend time together, we don't touch. We talk about the past throughout both evenings, but the stories we tell belong to the others.

Do you remember the time Nicky tried to cook risotto and the saucepan caught fire?

Howard and his pyjamas, folding them every morning, it was the unsexiest thing I've ever seen.

Sunetra's pot, it's still there, can you believe it? Dan still keeps a spare key in it.

This act of reliving it, filling in the memories between us to create a crude, piecemeal version of what was once our relationship, brings a level of closure I hadn't ever imagined I would get.

I feel done with it. The whole thing.

I'm glad Suscutin wasn't around back then. I'm glad I don't have to go on loving her. She has learned to quantify everything that I want to keep immeasurable. By the end of my time in her cosy flat, I'm certain that I loved her least of all too.

> • <

In the churchyard once more, there's a sense that so much time has passed since I was last here. How can that be? And yet my entire relationship, my Sixdom, has changed in my eyes, in my memory. I can't begin to articulate its alteration. I feel different, deep down different. I feel fresh, vulnerable. Ready to be made over.

I feel as if I've moulted.

I take up my position on the bench beside the church wall in the early morning, and they come in a steady stream, often in threes and fours, approaching without particular reverence. I watch them chat as they lay flowers in a fantail that radiates out from her grave, thickening and stretching wider and wider.

This isn't as I imagined it; they don't look like disciples. They gather, their numbers swelling, and they begin to talk louder about themselves. They turn their backs to the graves, and away from me.

I'm glad I hold my own bunch of flowers, carnations, and am wearing sunglasses, and dark trousers with my sharp shirt. I'm acting too, pretending to be properly bereaved so I can observe in peace. It's working. Some glance at me, but nobody pays me much attention.

The morning passes, and still they assemble; I hear raised voices outside the graveyard every now and again. How does this end? With a celebration, or a riot? A news crew arrives and pushes its way through to Petra's grave, training the eye of the camera on the flowers. The reporter, an older man, approaches one group. They speak animatedly to the lens, not to him. It's powerful to watch.

The crew, satisfied, leave. Midday approaches, and I'm starving. She isn't coming. She isn't coming. Why should she come? How would I know her, anyway?

I should go to Devon. I should check on Gwen, and help her move into the hospice with the duck pond, and simply tell her that she should forgive herself, if that's what it takes to be happy. I'm not cut out for this business of finding people and facilitating forgiveness.

The churchyard is packed, and the sun is hot; I'm sweating even in the shade of the wall. The voices outside are louder, more strident. Perhaps the sun is to blame. I heard once that crowd disturbances, riots, they mainly happen in summertime. Few rebel during rainfall nowadays.

Max could have silenced them. When he got annoyed on set, he used his trained voice to hold the crew to attention, but even he would have had trouble cutting through the police sirens that are drawing closer. There aren't small groups any more; there is a large crowd, and they are organising themselves, becoming more ordered in their outrage. The grave is forgotten entirely and the flower fantail is being trampled upon. I see people unfurl banners from their bags and shake them out, red paint on white cloth, and others unzip tops to reveal T-shirts underneath, bearing bold red lettering.

A young woman, maybe a student, approaches me and holds out a T-shirt. She gets dragged back by the others; I catch the use of the word disrespectful. Then she is parted from her friends by an older woman with a worn leather pack on her back, pushing through, using one arm out straight in front of her to divide the crowd. People move aside for her as she heads for Petra's grave.

She stands on other people's flowers, makes no attempt to avoid putting her feet upon them, and places one white rose on the top of the stone. She pats the marble with a familiar, weary gesture.

I remember her.

I saw her once, at Max's estate. He was filming, he broke off to speak to her, and we lost the light for the rest of the day. Nothing more could be shot. She stuck in my mind, perhaps because of the way he approached her, with a gentleness that was at odds with the control he exhibited on set.

Later, over beers in his luxurious living room, I said, 'This is going to take ages if you break off a shot to speak to every hanger-on.'

And he replied, 'How do you know she was a hanger-on? You're talking about the love of my fucking life, Mik.' Then he smiled, I smiled, and he dealt cards for poker. There was a beer ready for Gwen, placed on the table; she'd gone to do her last sweep of the house for the evening.

So here's the love of Max Black's life, the hanger-on, the person Gwen has to apologise to.

Rose Allington.

The crowd heave into action as my watch registers midday. As they stream from the graveyard she gets jostled. She bumps the white rose from its place upon the stone. I walk to it, retrieve it, replace it. The churchyard empties in a rush. They are off, striding, shouting, a sibilant mess of Suscutin-hating slogans, while through a loudspeaker I hear a man call for order.

Rose and I are alone.

'Thanks,' she says, but I can't hear it over the crowd; I read it from the shape of her thin lips. She looks very tired and very angry, red-cheeked and bleary-eyed. Time has not been kind to her; her skin has sagged, and her hair is brittle, dry.

I nod, to show I've understood, then wait until the crowd is far away enough so that I can be heard if I raise my voice. 'Petra would have hated this, wouldn't she?'

Rose frowns, but nods back.

'They're using her as an excuse.'

'You knew her?' she asks.

'No. I know what happens to people when they become famous. The way they have things hung upon them.'

I remove my sunglasses, and I see it – that familiar moment of realisation in their eyes. That recognition of who I am. Perhaps she's placed me at Max's estate that day, or from the Stuck Six stories, or even from that stupid skinny dip. I can't tell.

She steps away from me and lifts her arms up in front of her; it's a classic defensive position. Bodyguard training, perhaps.

'We've met before,' I say.

'No, I don't think so.'

'Well, we didn't meet. We were in the same place at the same time. Max Black was a mutual friend.'

'No, no, I've never, I didn't know him.'

'You're not a very good liar.'

She's breathing deeply. Dressed simply in jeans and a loose shirt, the straps of a small leather backpack pressing on her shoulders, she doesn't look like she could defend herself, let alone another human being. 'You're Mickey Stuck.'

'And you're Rose Allington.'

'My surname is Stacey, now,' she says, eventually.

The crowd is a raucous background to our conversation, but they're getting further away, and a measure of calm is returning to me now I've found her. 'I've never been that close to an angry mob before.'

'They've come every year since the fire. I shouldn't turn up at the same time, but… I don't want her to be alone with them, if that makes sense. They're not all a bad bunch. I've met worse.'

'People do strange things for causes they believe in.'

'In Petra's case, she just didn't like people getting away with bad behaviour.'

'Taking Suscutin leads to bad behaviour?'

'You're full of questions,' she says. 'And you tracked me down, right? What's this for? The follow-up documentary about your film? Or just to find your own answers? You should be a private investigator. I could get you set up with a job interview.'

'You were a detective?' She looks wrong for that role, as well: too nervous, too honest.

She narrows her eyes at me. 'Well, now I'm intrigued. You don't know a thing about me, but here you are. Why is that?'

Here goes. 'I have a request. On behalf of a close friend, who wants to apologise to you. In person.'

'Who's that?'

'She's dying. She just wants to say sorry. I don't know any more than that. But I promised her I would find you and ask you.'

'Who?'

'Gwen Taylor.'

'Who?' Then the last name seems to stick, and she doesn't even bother to say no; she simply walks away from me, taking a random path across the grass and around the back of the church, stepping around the gravestones.

I follow, keeping a little distance, as she circles the church to arrive at the entrance. I think she'll go inside, but she turns away and strides from the graveyard instead. I keep my eyes on her bobbing backpack as she crosses the main road and squeezes between two parked police cars to take a side street that leads to a car park I didn't know existed.

It's full, every space taken by cars with stickers bearing the slogan

BAN SUSCUTIN
Love the skin you're in

displayed in windows. She stops next to one of those new electric cars and produces the key from her pocket.

'Hey!' I call, and she freezes in place. She doesn't look at me as I approach.

'She's my friend, and she's dying,' I say. 'Wouldn't you do the same?'

'Just like Max was your friend, right?'

'Yeah.'

'I touched your skin,' she says, and she looks me straight in the eye, with an intensity, a knowledge, that brings a prickle of shame to my skin. 'In the British Museum. You helped get Max's film finished, didn't you?'

'I did.'

'Is it truthful?'

I raise my chin and bear her stare. 'More so than anything else people have said about me.'

'I went to see it. It was nothing like the autobiography.'

'No.' Honesty compels me to add, 'Howard is many things, but he's not much of a writer.'

'It was beautiful. I don't understand how Max could have made it, at that time. He was so… damaged. By then.'

'No, he wasn't damaged.'

'And then he just committed suicide out of the blue, is that what you're saying?'

'For fuck's sake.' My anger, my shame, she's coaxing it out

of me; fine, she can have it. 'For fuck's sake! Just tell me. Just tell me.'

She flinches. She's scared of me. My voice reverberates, then dies away. The march of the protestors is background noise; they must be at the laboratory gates by now. I'm an idiot, a loud one, and this shame won't go away.

'I'm sorry.'

'I still don't understand it,' she says. 'That wonderful film. Are you proud of it?'

'Very.' I could add, it feels like the only thing I've ever done entirely right.

'And you think you know Max well? Knew him, I mean.'

That's a much more difficult question. I tell her, 'There are things that happened. Nobody will talk to me about it. I think I could have helped, if I had known. I could have been a better friend.' My shame is so heavy now, I squirm under the weight of it, and under the weight of her even gaze. 'Please, just come with me. Hear her apology, and be done with it.'

'I can't be done with it by listening to Taylor telling me she's sorry. But I'll make a deal with you. Come with me now, and talk to me. About the Max you knew, and your life. Then you can ask me whatever you want, and I'll answer it. And if you really still want me to forgive Taylor then I'll let you try and persuade me.'

This is what I wanted, isn't it? This is what I've really been searching for. Somebody laying out all the things that were hidden.

Why, then, does it take such an effort of will to get into the passenger seat, and stay there while she sits in the driver's seat and starts the car? The fear I felt in the graveyard returns, redoubles.

She is driving, and I don't know where we're going.
This is happening right now. This is out of my control.

PART FOUR

SATURDAY, 20 JULY 2022, 5:42PM.

Mik: This is your house?

Rose: It's not far from the Clifton Suspension Bridge, actually. I have family near here. I run a design business.

Mik: Are you recording this? Is that why your phone's on the table?

Rose: It's nothing. It's just for my memory. Things have a way of changing when I look back on them. I thought this might help me to keep it straight. In my head.

Mik: I'm not comfortable with it.

<Pause>

Rose: You don't have to do this. This is entirely your choice.

Mik: I'm happy to talk to you, just not—

Rose: It's for me. I won't sell it. I won't play it to anyone else. You'll have to trust me. Tell me about Taylor.

Mik: She has – uh – epidermal sclerosis.

Rose: The skin condition? The one that's being linked to Suscutin?

Mik: There's no proof of that yet.

Rose: <laughter>

Mik: You think it's funny?

Rose: It's ironic, I'll give it that.

Mik: She's dying.

Rose: So you said. She's dying, she's your friend. Tell me something. Tell me about the first time you met her. Was it through Max?

<Pause>

Mik: Are you sure you need to record it?

Rose: You can walk away. There's the door. I'll even call

you a taxi, if you like. Go back and tell her you didn't find me, if it makes you feel better.

Mik: No, okay. Yeah. I met her and Max at the same time. It was about a year after we broke up. The Sixes, I mean.

Rose: Okay. Tell me. Tell me like it's a story.

2012. GIVE THE MAN A CARD.

He was the only other Stuck to make it to the party.

Howard was there, of course, in the centre of a group who were hanging on his words; he winked and waved when he caught sight of Mik, and Mik smiled back. He hadn't objected to the autobiography, and certainly appreciated even more money. He had become a wealthy man, no longer reliant on his father's generosity, and he was standing in the centre of an exclusive London venue, high above the city lights.

If he had a misgiving, it was about the way their lives had been presented in the book. The events had gained a sheen of romantic inevitability, every moment foreshadowing the moment of the first moult, rather like one might find in a fairy tale. It all made too much sense, at the cost of reality. But this was an easy objection to put aside, considering the benefits. Frankly, Mik was surprised the others hadn't seen it that way too.

He suspected they would come around in their own time. They had all said yes to the donation of their old skins to the British Museum; that had been Sunetra's idea. He thought it a vain, ridiculous gesture but didn't have the heart to veto it with everyone else in rare agreement.

Living art, she had said down the phone to him.

If he had been in the mood to puncture her enthusiasm for her latest idea he would have pointed out it was merely dead skin, and irrelevant to the living.

He made his way to the free bar, a creation of chrome and spotlights close to the glass wall, and ordered a beer.

'Not drinking champagne?' said a voice, on his right, and he recognised the famous, very handsome, profile.

'It gives me mood swings,' he said, trying to sound cool and instantly hating what he had just said. He'd met quite a few famous people since becoming a celebrity himself, but this – this was stardom personified.

'I thought maybe it was because you weren't celebrating.'

'You've read the book, then?'

'I've done more than that,' said Max Black. 'I've already bought the rights.'

'The rights?' Mik said, then realised what it meant. 'Fuck, really? A film?'

'That's the plan. I'm getting into directing.'

'Fuck.' Howard hadn't even mentioned it. Maybe he thought there would be no objection from him; it was yet more money. Probably a vast amount of money. But it was uncomfortable in a way he couldn't immediately process. It had something to do with the difference between words on a page and images on a screen; there was less room for interpretation of events, perhaps.

'You're not pleased,' Max said. 'Listen, I'm sorry. How come Howard holds all the rights?'

'It was easier to give control to just one of us, back when it all kicked off. Plus – and I'm aware this is a trite line – we were in love.'

'If it makes you feel any better, he's making you rich.'

'Actually, it does,' said Mik. 'Beats the hell out of not being rich.'

Max laughed. 'I bet it does. This is Taylor. She's a fan of yours.'

The tall blonde in a severe suit, standing just behind Max's shoulder, said, 'Shut up, Max,' in an even tone, and went back to surveying the room.

'She's a keen bodyguard, but an even keener Stuck-Chick.'

'I hate that phrase,' Mik said. There were as many male fans as female fans of the Six phenomenon; Mik had no idea why only the women got that derogatory nickname, and seemed to revel in it.

'Me too,' said Taylor. 'Use it again and I'll break your nose.'

'She's new,' said Max, 'but I really like her already.'

'Listen, the book is true, I mean, it's correct about a lot of stuff that happened. But it's from Howard's point of view.'

Max raised an eyebrow. 'You're saying it's different from your point of view?'

'Everything is different from every point of view, isn't it?'

'True. That's difficult to film, though.'

Mik shrugged. 'Isn't it a perfect subject to try with?' He finished his beer, and ordered another. 'Drink?'

Max shook his head. 'I have to get going. It was good to meet you, though.'

'You too.'

'Maybe – I'd like to get some thoughts about the direction the film will take – we could get together and talk it over? If you're interested in getting your point of view up there as well.'

'Sounds good.'

'Taylor, give the man a card.'

The blonde reached into her suit pocket and produced a cream-coloured business card. Mik pocketed it, and she wrinkled her nose up at him, just for a moment; it was an endearing bunny-rabbit gesture at total odds with her persona.

'See?' said Max. 'She only does that with the cute ones.

Not with me.'

'You're not my type,' she said to her employer.

'You should talk to the others,' said Mik. 'Get their perspectives too. I can put you in touch, if you'd like.'

'No thanks,' said Max. 'I've already tried them. They all said no.'

So it was a set-up, the whole thing; Max was there to meet him, to engineer a response in him, and he had the feeling Taylor was there for that reason too: to reel him in. And it had worked; it had flattered him, intrigued him. He had already made up his mind to phone the number, and get involved.

Later, after Max and Taylor had gone and Mik had given up trying to be social in favour of getting drunk and staring out over the lights of London, Howard came up behind him, and softly said, 'Hey you.'

They hugged. Mik clung on to the familiar cushiony form of his old lover, feeling a deep nostalgia for that house they had shared on the edge of Grafham Water, and the way Howard had taken him, cherished him, managed him.

But after a brief, petulant conversation about the film rights it became obvious that everything they could say to each other would lead to disagreement at best and a shouting match at worst. If he was going to shout at any of them, it would be Howard, who always thought he was in control but cried easily and satisfyingly. Mik said goodbye, and left the party. It looked like it would happily go on all night without him.

SATURDAY, 20 JULY 2022, 6:57PM.

Mik: I should find a hotel or something.

Rose: I told you, stay here. Can you concentrate now, please, because I'm recording again.

Mik: You were his bodyguard? Max's?

Rose: For a while.

<Pause>

Mik: You were lovers?

Rose: For a while.

Mik: He told me once you were the love of his life.

Rose: He told me that too.

Mik: You didn't believe him? He didn't seem to be a womaniser.

Rose: I don't know what love is any more.

<Pause>

Rose: Tell me what love is. To you.

Mik: To me? That's impossible.

Rose: Tell me how love starts. Can you do that? How does love between six people start? It was all for the papers, wasn't it? It couldn't have been real. I touched the skins. They felt... artificial.

Mik: Didn't you read the information sheet before you went in? The museum had all the skins treated with a fixative, to preserve them. It can alter the way it feels.

Rose: No. I didn't see that.

Mik: It was real. I promise you. It didn't happen all at once, though. I fell for them one at a time, and they accepted me into their lives. Quite quickly, actually.

Rose: So which one was first for you?

2009. FAST LEARNER.

'Speak Russian to me,' said Nicky.

They had grabbed the two seats just in front of the luggage rack, being quick to board the stopper train, and with the aisle now filled with standing students there was an illusion of privacy in their position. She had her hand on his knee; it was difficult to concentrate.

'I think maybe I love you,' Mik said, in his old language, enjoying that she wouldn't understand it.

She shivered, an accentuated jostle of her shoulders, for effect. 'It's a beautiful language.'

'You're weird, did I tell you that?'

'Do you miss speaking it?'

'Not really. But I'm glad to speak it to you if it makes you happy.'

She held a fascination for him. It was the grace of her, the languid nature of her movements juxtaposed with that sharp brain, and her ability to win any verbal argument in minutes, particularly when it came to English literature. And yet, perhaps because of his Russian birth, she submitted to him when he spoke, and never contradicted him directly. If she did disagree with something he said, she did it with a light touch of humour. He felt such touches as marks upon his skin, and was beginning to think they were sinking through the layers to impregnate him.

'I hope I like them,' he said, in Russian. 'And I hope they like me.'

'More,' she said.

The train slowed, and stopped at Five Ways. Students

streamed from the aisle, down on to the platform. Five more stops to go.

'Do you think they'll like me? Isn't this sort of an affair?'

'Don't be nervous. They're fine about it. It's not a possessive thing.'

'It feels creepy.' A group of five, living together in love. She had asked him not to tell anyone, and he hadn't, but he felt as if it might have helped to describe it to somebody else. What words would he use? A commune? A gang-bang? A live-in orgy? Years in a British boarding school, sent there on the behest of his rich Anglophile father after his first moult, had given him enough language to have a few descriptive alternatives for Nicky's arrangement, but none of them quite seemed to fit.

'Mik,' said a voice from the aisle; in the shuffling after the first set of departures from the carriage, a fellow student from his Business Management course had ended up standing beside him. 'Did you take notes for Clark's two o'clock on Organisational Behaviour?'

'Yeah. I'll be in the library tomorrow morning, if you want to have a look.'

'Great, thanks.'

He wanted to get Nicky to run through all the names and personalities he would be meeting again, but the presence of the student – whose name he couldn't even remember at that moment – stymied him. It was only after the next stop, and the desertion of another raft of bodies while others fitted themselves into the freed seats, that the aisle was clear and Mik felt able to ask.

She rattled the names off, and provided neat little descriptions that amused him, including exact details such as a favourite film or a predilection for olives. They passed out of his head upon the instant of hearing them.

'And you really love all of them?'

'Yeah. I can't explain it. We all bring something different to it. I don't have to be everything to one person. It relieves the pressure.'

'But would you love them if they came as individuals?'

She thought about that for a while, her hand still on his knee. 'I don't know. I met Howard and Liz first. They were a couple, and I rented a room from them in my second year at uni. Sunetra was already living there, and then I realised they were all together, and I guess I fell for Sunetra, and it grew from there. Then Dan came to mend the boiler one day.'

'That is bizarre,' said Mik. 'It's amazing, though. I've never heard of anything like it before, not in Russia, not here. Does it happen a lot, do you think, secretly?' He often felt that life was not exactly how it was represented to him by the older generation, and suspected one day he would discover the real facts that everybody else was already in on.

She shook her head. 'Only in romantic literature. But all those stories end in tragedy.'

He changed the subject after that. The next three stops passed through Birmingham's centre; the students left and the shoppers boarded, and by the time they got to Erdington he felt a little ashamed of his long, loose hair and tight, ripped jeans. Nicky, in a flowing skirt and sky-blue top, swept slowly from the train, and she left a trail of lavender for him to follow.

He had complimented her on her perfume when they first met. It had been at a drama club audition for roles in a turgid play of skin atrocities and pornography written by one of the postgraduates. The declamatory style insisted upon by the director got them both giggling, and later, in the Union bar, she had told him that she took a bath every night, dropping lavender essence in the water. If it had been a deliberate come-on, it had seriously worked. He had pictured her alone, soaping a leg in her tiny student-rental bathroom, but now he wondered – does she bathe alone? Perhaps they had an enormous decadent tub and washed each other's backs.

But walking through Erdington, in Nicky's aromatic wake, it seemed to Mik that it was not the kind of place to hold a vast palace in which the five of them lived. She stopped on the street outside one house in an unremarkable row of tall houses with steep sloping roofs, and squeezed between two cars parked close, bumper to bumper, in a long line of cars that all faced the same way.

'Here we are,' she said, and took his hand to lead him inside.

The immediate impression was of unseen activity. 'Want a drink?' called a man from the end of the hallway, and a woman immediately shouted, 'Tea please!' from upstairs. The man appeared, a blue mug in hand. He was dressed in a business suit and wore a gold tie, loosened at the knot. He was heavy-set, his fingers meaty around the mug, and his sandy brown hair was unkempt. Mik felt a surge of awareness. I know him. I will know him.

'I wasn't talking to you!' the man called back up the stairs, but he was smiling. 'Right. Coffee, Nick?'

'Yep,' said Nicky. 'And Mik drinks coffee too.'

'Milk? Sugar?'

'Both,' said Mik.

'I'm Howard.'

'He knows that,' Nicky said, rolling her eyes, and the dynamic of the house felt so clear to Mik in that moment, sketched perfectly in this first meeting with daily life, small actions given and taken, teasing and talking, knowing each other so well. Surely this was the ideal way to have a relationship; it was so different from his parents' dry silences, long after moulting had taken place but they had made the decision to not ask for anything further from love. But here was an excess of love, and it was risky, and beautiful for that. When their skins loosened it would fall away.

It would be worth it, though. To have felt so cherished, and to have that memory. Yes, it would be worth it.

'We're just popping upstairs,' said Nicky.

'Cool,' Howard said. He couldn't have been more than twenty-five, but he acted like a much older man. Perhaps it was the suit. 'I'll leave the coffees outside the door. Don't let them get cold.'

'Right.'

'Dinner at seven,' he called, as she pulled Mik up the stairs, and another smiling face craned around a door on the landing, and murmured something that he didn't catch; this woman's eyes were bright, calculating, and her close-cut black hair caught his attention.

'Hello,' she said.

He felt the same pull to her, too – as if he already had knowledge about her, about what was going to happen next.

Before he could speak Nicky pulled him up the next flight of stairs and into the first room on the right. It was wood-panelled, the ceiling sloping, a skylight letting the sun pour through on to the double bed, giving it a hot, close feeling like a sauna.

She took a 'Do Not Disturb' sign from the small bedside table and hung it on the door before closing it.

'Is this your room?' he asked. It was impersonal, undecorated.

'We don't have rooms. We just have signs when we want to be left alone. Like, right now. I want to be left alone with you.'

She undressed him, pulled down his tight jeans before he had removed his shoes, and left him in an awkward tangle, which seemed to take ages to sort out. It was, crazily, the first time he had been alone with her. It felt to him that she and her companions, fate included, were rushing him along to a preordained destination.

But it felt good. The speed of the journey, and the hands that wanted to hold him, bring him along, as they travelled.

She finished removing his clothes and then reached up under her skirt to remove her knickers, placing them on the bedside table.

'You're mine for now,' she said, 'just for now,' and knelt on the bed, gathering up the folds of her skirt to her waist.

'I don't know if I can—' he said, but it was a lie and he was already hard. He knelt face to face with her, crushing the material of the skirt between their upper bodies, and found her so eager for the taste of his skin, her lips finding his shoulder, sucking at his neck, moaning without shame of being overheard.

When he heard Howard's steps on the stairs, measured, deliberately loud, he timed his strokes to each footfall. And

the placing of the mugs, and the soft knock on the door –
that was when he came, his senses filled with the house, the
presences who were listening to their fucking, who would
be part of it if he let them, and if they wanted him. He was
desperate for them to want him.

SATURDAY, 20 JULY 2022, 7:31PM.

Rose: So it was about the sex, for you?

Mik: Of course it was about the sex. I was nineteen years old. We were all under twenty-five. Sex was a huge part of it. It was also the part that got the press hot under the collar. That's how we came to their attention, actually. One of Nicky's conquests had a brother who worked for a newspaper.

Rose: Nicky had other lovers?

Mik: She was in love with us. She fucked other people on a regular basis. She used protection and we understood it, as a need. Sex is just sex. It was the least interesting thing about us, in a way.

Rose: The film glossed over that part.

Mik: I said, it's not that interesting. Plus the other producers wanted a 12 rating. What is it you want to know? We rarely did it as a big group. That stuff just looks good for porn movies but somebody always ends up feeling left out. Usually we did it in twos or threes, depending on who we felt close to. That changed all the time. Personal preferences are none of your business, no matter how much you threaten me over Gwen.

<Pause>

Rose: You make me sound like a monster. I thought this was give and take. I help you, you help me, you know. I'm not, you're not—

Mik: I know. I can leave at any time.

<Pause>

Rose: So that's it. I've become a monster now. I get it. Perhaps it was bound to happen. But I need to know, it's been years of not knowing, I didn't realise how it would feel, and then Petra died because of me, because of my problems—

Mik: She tried to stop Suscutin production because of you?

Rose: Did you know Max was one of the original investors in Suscutin? He took it for years. Long before it passed regulations. He gave it to me too. As an early guinea pig.

<Pause>

Mik: Why you?

Rose: That's difficult to explain. Love does strange things to people. Perhaps the easiest way to explain it is to say that I have Extreme Moult Syndrome.

Mik: EMS? I heard Suscutin cures that.

Rose: I didn't want to be cured. I still don't. Max thought I should be whether I liked it or not.

Mik: He didn't want you to suffer.

Rose: There are worse things in life than suffering. You fell in love, all six of you. You knew it would hurt when it ended. Knowing hurt is always coming, is only ever one layer of skin away, is not some evolutionary mistake. It happens for a reason.

Mik: I've heard that argument before, but it sounds a bit too close to a religion for my liking.

Rose: Losing your skin is not the tragedy at the heart of the human condition. Feeling the same way forever, that's the worst.

<Pause>

Mik: So Petra agreed with you, about the tragedy of the human condition, as you call it. She tried to burn down the Suscutin laboratories because of it.

Rose: No. I don't know what she felt about Suscutin.

I asked her to burn it down, and she tried. She'd done it before. She was good at getting rid of things and people that shouldn't be allowed to exist.

Mik: Who are you to make that call?

Rose: She burned down empty office blocks that were being used to hold skin fights between trafficked slaves, and she burned down houses where teenaged girls were being groomed to fall in love with men who would then flay off their skin in videos. She burned down factories that specialised in clothes made from— look, however young and untouched you are, you can't claim there's any grey area here.

Mik: I, I— Yes, the world can be a horrible place, I know that, I know that. I'm sorry you've seen stuff like that.

Rose: That's not the point. Don't make it about me. This is about you. You helping Taylor, when she deserves some sort of justice.

Mik: Is that what your friend Petra provided? Justice?

<Pause>

Rose: Petra tried to help me, just as you keep trying to help Taylor. What makes her so special? What makes her worthy of your help?

Mik: I made her a promise.

2013. FLUSH.

'You've just insulted the love of my fucking life,' said Max, and smiled. He dealt the cards, flicking them across the green baize of the tabletop.

Mik smiled back, although he didn't know why. Was it a joke? Nothing Max said could ever quite be believed; working together on the script and now spending time together during the shooting process had taught him that. Max liked to manufacture moments, saying or doing things for effect, even when there were only the two of them present. The mystery of him – the idea that somewhere under the Hollywood persona there was something more meaningful and less pretty that stayed smothered under the unrelenting need for personal perfection – was one of the things Mik liked best about his new friend. It was a battle he had fought himself, when the papers started to construct their own narrative of him as the toy-boy of the Stuck Six.

But it did make Max difficult to trust. Mik couldn't spend long periods of time with him, in case he lost his own reality, so hard fought for. So he had refused the offer of a room of his own in Max's Sussex mansion, and had instead opted for a trailer on the grounds once filming started. It gave him distance, and a space of his own. He found he needed that so much more after living as one of the Six. He struggled with concepts of his own possessions, and what sorts of embellishments he should make to his own living area; it was difficult to be totally responsible for himself and his surroundings, but necessary.

Friends were also necessary. Uncomplicated friends, if

such a thing existed. If not – fuck it. Beer and poker, and a damaged superstar for company.

The third hand of cards sat next to a beer, before the seat Gwen always took, facing the door. Max regularly dealt her in whether she was present or not; he seemed reliant on the idea that they came as a team and her protection extended over him. She, in turn, insulted him in public, and was an attentive, maternal figure when it was just the three of them. Mik couldn't imagine what they were like when they were alone – soulmates who discussed everything, or an old married couple who rarely exchanged words?

They played a few warm-up hands until Gwen arrived, her cheeks red.

'It's all clear,' she said.

Max checked his watch. 'That usually makes it – yup. Time for meds.' He left the games room as she unbuttoned her jacket and draped it over the back of her chair. He took medication every night, and often sent Gwen out to fetch it. Mik never raised it as a subject. If it was an ongoing illness, a skin condition maybe, it wouldn't have fitted with Max's carefully guarded self-image and he never would have told the truth about it to another person anyway.

Gwen took a sip of her beer. 'It's really warm in here.'

'No, it's just cold outside tonight.' But she was right, the room was very warm, the windows shut up tight and the green silk walls oppressive. It was not to Mik's taste, but he supposed it was a traditional take on a games room, with a snooker table, and its own bar in matching mahogany with a row of optics to match. Above it, there was a painting of a chestnut horse with a sturdy body and elongated legs that Mik found disturbing, as if reality had skewed.

'I'm really tired,' Gwen said.

'You okay?'

'Yeah. Fine. I could have done without the cross-examination over my working methods today, that's all.'

'Who was that? The woman who was asking you about stuff earlier?'

'Forget it,' she said, and took another sip from her beer. 'Listen, we get on well, right?'

'Yeah.' She was matter-of-fact, always serious with him, giving lots of eye contact in a way that seemed to him to be a plea for honesty on his part. It led Mik to think that she was very honest with him, as an act of reciprocity.

'Do you think we only get on because of Max? Like, he's the linking factor?'

'If that was true,' Mik said, 'it would be really awkward every time he left the room. Which he does a lot. And, to be honest, I quite look forward to those moments.'

'Me too,' she said.

'Okay, so what is it?'

'Do you think love is very different from friendship?'

'Wow. I wasn't expecting that. Um… Yeah. It's different. You can feel it. In the skin.'

'I've never been in love,' she said.

'I've been in love a lot.'

'I don't want to be in love. Ever. It causes so many problems.'

He took a swallow of his beer, and said, 'That sounds like a bad childhood talking.'

'Not at all. I just— I'm content. As I am. I wish everyone could be.'

'Do you mean Max?' said Mik.

She nodded, and leaned back in her seat. 'He's my responsibility. He's so desperate to try to understand love. Through the Stuck Six, through his own experiences. I wish I could get him to give up on the whole thing. All his plans and projects.'

'What, like the film?'

'Yes, like the film. Like anything do to with love. All his crazy ideas. He spends so much money, he wastes so much time.'

'We should start a celibacy club.'

'Are you celibate?' she asked him, all astonishment.

'Aren't you?'

'God, no. I just don't ever confuse love and sex.'

'You get laid? What, a lot? When? With who?'

'That's my business.'

He didn't believe it. 'Well, you're not responsible for Max, or his happiness.'

'Maybe not, but when I took this job I decided I was going to do the best I can. And that involves doing whatever it takes to help him.'

It was a ridiculous statement, casting herself as his nurse, mother, friend and manager. What a pairing they were: the handsome actor/director who lived in a land of his own imagination, and the very serious bodyguard who was determined to let him.

And what did he bring to it all? He couldn't think of a thing, apart from being there when the pieces inevitably needed to be picked up. 'Well,' he said, 'how about in that case I'll do the best I can to help you, if you ever need it. Deal?'

'Deal.'

'I thought I already dealt,' said Max, from the doorway, and Gwen said, 'Oh, shut up and sit down.'

So Max did, and the game began.

SATURDAY, 20 JULY 2022, 9:14PM.

Mik: —understand why there was no trace of you. I had investigators on it.

Rose: Petra had some talented friends in… unusual lines of work. After she died they came to me, told me she'd asked them to change my name and alter my records if anything went wrong. I think she was worried the Suscutin lot would come after me.

Mik: Seriously?

Rose: You're sweet. Weirdly innocent about life. Which bit don't you believe? That people would want to protect a multi-billion-pound industry, or that other people would be able to protect me from them? Well, maybe you're right. I'm not sure anybody ever did come looking for me. Until you. Why should they bother? I've learned my lesson.

<Pause>

Mik: So… why are you recording again?

Rose: Another question for you.

Mik: And then you'll tell me what I need to know?

<Pause>

Mik: That was the deal, right?

Rose: I know, I just… Are you sure you want to know? I find I'm reluctant to destroy that innocence.

Mik: If it's not a deal then stop recording.

Rose: No. It's still a deal.

Mik: Okay. So what else can I tell you about Gwen to make you realise she's not the devil? She likes disco music. She's rubbish at poker because she always looks delighted when she gets a good hand. She reads a lot of books, big fantasy books, you know, thirty-eight in a never-ending series-so-far books.

Rose: Not about Taylor. About Max. Tell me about the last time you saw him.

Mik: No, I don't think so.

Rose: Why? Did you argue?

Mik: No. It won't give you what you want, that's all. Nothing happened. It was a normal conversation about filming, and you don't want that, do you? I'll give you what you want. What will satisfy you.

Rose: No, I don't want—

Mik: Listen.

2013. THAT'S WHAT FRIENDS ARE FOR.

'I've done something terrible.'

She stood back from the steps that led to the door of the trailer; Mik could look down on the crown of her blond hair, for once. Her arms were crossed, and her shoulders raised, defensive.

'What's up?'

'I have to get out of here.'

'Is Max all right?' His first thought was that she'd had to confront an intruder, maybe even tackle them personally. But the more Mik looked at her, the more he could see that it was not adrenaline running through her, but some deep emotion she was trying to contain.

'He's fine, he's not— The best thing for everyone is if I get away from him, and stay away. I shouldn't be near him. I make everything worse.'

The other trailers were dotted about the long flat section of grass in this part of Max's estate, but as work had been halted for the last few days most people had taken the opportunity to go home or go to London. Still, Mik felt self-conscious, standing above her, meeting her eyes at this angle. 'Come in,' he said, and quickly threw the remains of the ready meal he'd had for a late Sunday lunch into the bin in the cupboard under the sink.

He had discovered a fondness for trailer living, which enclosed him and yet demanded no permanence from him, but he hated others to see it, pass judgement on him because of it. Gwen looked around the small, messy space – his film magazines and dirty crockery – but didn't seem to care. She sat on one side of the padded bench that ran around the tabletop, and he closed the door quietly, then sat opposite. 'Tell me what's wrong.'

She didn't even respond to that. 'Look, I wouldn't ask, but you said...'

'I know, I know. I meant it, you were right to come here. What do you need?'

'A ride. Don't ask me what happened. Don't ever tell Max where I am.'

'Fuck,' he said.

'Can you do that?'

He heard a different question underneath. The question of whether he really was her friend.

It was Dan who popped into his head. Dan, and his decision to help Mik leave when all the others were determined to make him stay. It's still love, Howard had said, over and over, just in a different form, not in the skin, but we can make it work, if you'll only try harder. It had been Dan's money, Dan's contacts, Dan's understanding, Dan's unconditional help that had saved him.

'Yes,' he said. 'I can do that.'

He grabbed his phone, wallet and car keys and took her hand as they left the trailer, heading back across the grass in the afternoon sunlight. Her palm was clammy, her grip strong – what couldn't Gwen, amazing Gwen, possibly face? Didn't she know she could overcome anything? What had Max done to rob her of her control? She stared up at the house as it came into view, her gaze fearful; he thought she was looking at the windows, checking to see if Max appeared.

She was afraid of seeing him.

That couldn't be right.

'Did Max... touch you?' he said, grasping at straws.

'Do you think I'd let him?' she said, and he saw a trace of the Gwen he knew well, and was relieved.

'In that case, surely we can sort it out. It's probably just a miscommunication. Nothing could be that bad. Nothing is unforgiveable between friends, right?'

She didn't answer.

They veered off to the left, to Max's enormous car park with its painted white lines and gleaming vehicles. Mik unlocked his BMW, and Gwen tucked herself into the passenger seat, sliding down low as they pulled away. He drove them out of the estate with only a perfunctory wave from the security guard at the gate.

'Where do you want to go?'

'Devon,' she said.

'Really?'

'I went there a few times as a kid. The north coast. I know it, a little.'

'You got enough money for a hotel down there? Until this blows over?'

'It's not a whim, Mik.'

'No, I meant – I'm sorry. You will need money, though, won't you? Think it through.'

'Okay. Yes. I'll need money. But—'

'Well then. I have money.'

'No, I don't want…'

'Shut up. It's just money. I have it, more than I need. I always wanted to get into property. Listen, I'll buy a house down there and you'll live in it for me. You can help me choose it. Think investment potential. From a bodyguard to a live-in housekeeper and portfolio manager in one day. Come on, let's do it.'

'You're mental,' she said, but she was smiling, and she didn't say no. It was a wild gamble, an attempt to make an adventure, but why not? That was the great blessing of money. And when she was ready to make up with Max, and for it to be the three of them again, he would know exactly where she was. He would keep her safe.

'What kind of house did you stay in before? In Devon?'

'It was a rental cottage in a village. Just a pub and a post office. No television. We stayed in the same place every year. I used to read so many books. Stories I could escape into. Then go and walk along the cliff paths. It never changed. I hope it still hasn't.'

'Cottage. Pub. Post office. Cliffs. Room for books. Got it.'

'Mental,' she said, again.

Mik's phone rang. The dashboard displayed the name—

MAX

'Don't,' she said.

'Gwen, I should just—'

'No. No.'

'Okay,' Mik said. 'Okay, okay,' until she was calm again.

Max rang four more times on the journey to Devon, and then fell silent.

There was a B&B in Lynmouth that was, Gwen said with great emotion, just the same. He gave her what cash he had in his wallet and then handed over one of his credit cards. He told her he'd be back in a couple of days to start house hunting with her.

'Are you going back to Max's?' she said.

'Of course. I won't mention you.' Max would, no doubt,

tell him everything. But with a gloss upon it. An argument? A hare-brained scheme that had backfired? Mik had considered all permutations. Nothing fit.

The room in which they stood had a large bay window that looked out over a valley; he crossed to it, and was rewarded with a view of a fat, slow river winding through boulders below, and an astonishing mass of greenery – an explosion of natural beauty. Gwen came to stand beside him.

'Thank you,' she said.

'I can see why you like this place.' But it would have been too quiet for him; he already knew that.

'It's not fair,' she whispered.

'What isn't? Tell me. Just tell me.'

'The last time we came here I was thirteen. We had a brilliant week. My mother, my stepfather and me. When we got back home he moulted. He left that night. We never saw him again. End of happy families. Then I moulted for the first time the week after, the week after, God, everything was suddenly so different. I was different. I couldn't bear it. I wanted it all back, to have it back, to have that one thing and for it to last.'

'You're my friend. Friendship lasts. It's not love. It's not even the Bond.'

'You chose me over Max. I know how much that will cost you,' she said, and then told him she was very tired, and wished him a safe journey back, so formally, like a grand lady saying her goodbyes at the end of a party.

'Gwen,' he said, before she could shut the door on him. 'It's okay. You're still you and I'm still me.'

'Not really,' she said, and then he left her, and began the long drive away from a magnificent sunset over the sea.

He tried to reach Max, ringing every half an hour. There was no answer.

Back at the estate, the gates were standing open, unattended, and there were so many people, uniforms, at the top of the gravel driveway, with the blue lights of the police cars and the ambulances flashing, flashing, flashing.

SATURDAY, 20 JULY 2019, 10:05PM.

Rose: You couldn't have known. You didn't know a thing about it. Why he took all those pills. You still don't know, do you? Taylor never told you. It's not your fault.

Mik: He called me. I didn't answer.

Rose: You did your best. You couldn't help them both.

Mik: I don't get it. Why I had to make a choice between them. But I made it, and I've stuck to it. Whatever Gwen did, I didn't falter. That's a good friend, right?

Rose: Yes. Absolutely.

Rose turns off her phone. 'I'm done recording,' she says. She wears a deep frown. I get the sense she's profoundly troubled by the things I've told her.

I get up from the sofa, stiff from sitting still for so long, and take a slow walk around her living room. On the mantelpiece, above an unlit wood burner, there are matching candlesticks holding white tapering candles. They look like they've never been lit. There are two silver-framed photographs, too. One shows the Eiffel Tower. The other shows Rose, not much younger than she is now I'd guess, with a toddler on her lap. There's a sky-blue background behind them both; it looks like a happy holiday memory.

'You've got a family?'

'Just Ethan,' she says. 'My late miracle. He's six now. He's with his dad this weekend.'

'You're on good terms with his dad?'

'Yes, fine. I was never in love with him, so that simplifies things. I've learned how to stay friends with people over the years.'

'Yeah,' I say. 'Friends.'

How pathetic these words are: sex, love, friend. How little they describe.

'I've spent years trying to understand myself,' she says. 'I've even tried writing it down. I described myself in the third person, past tense. She did this. She did that. She fell in love. She became a student. An administrator. A bodyguard. An investigator. A designer. It never all adds up to one person. One complete person, not in the way Max was complete. But now I'm beginning to think that's how it's meant to be. To be otherwise is either a lie or insanity.'

'I don't know. All I know is I keep looking for the truth.'

'You think it will make a difference?'

'How could I ever know that until I hear it?'

'All right then,' she says. 'I'll tell you my truth. I'll tell you what they did to me, and you can decide what they are, and what I am.'

It's getting late. I could easily tell her to leave it until the morning, or even later still. Or never. I've lived life in the easy territory of not knowing for so long.

I return to the sofa. She's composed, and ready to speak.

'Just tell me,' I say. 'Tell me now.'

2022. **BUSINESS.**

Gwen's right. The duck pond is restful. Insects skim across the surface, and the ducks dally, dive, resurface to create concentric circles, radiating out from their activities. It's a sunny afternoon in Devon, and she's picked a good place to wait to die.

Her pain is managed, but her papery face is still lined with it. I watch her nod as Rose talks to her.

They sit on a bench together, opposite me, the pond between us. I have been keeping my distance, pretending to look at the view, or to smell the roses that line the path. I have been taking very small steps around the paths to give them time.

There are many sufferers of Epidermal Sclerosis here; I have greeted some on my walk, and tried not to wince in sympathy at their diseased skin, crumpled and hanging, losing its shape.

I understand now how Rose could say there was a certain irony to Gwen's condition. I also see how she could refuse, even after all I told her, to provide forgiveness on demand.

In the end I didn't ask her to. Some things really are unforgiveable, but whether Gwen's decision to help Max commit those acts of violence, of horror, is one of them is up to her, not me.

I only asked her to come with me to this hospice, that's all, and to set eyes on Gwen. To breathe the same air as her.

Rose made the move, made her own decision, to sit beside her on the bench.

I've done something terrible, Gwen said, and she was right about that too. I was arrogant to assume she was incapable of a terrible act. I robbed her of an essential part of herself, and she spent years living on my money, in my house, trying so hard to be the person I wanted her to be.

Enough.

I walk back to the bench, and Rose makes eye contact with me. She stands. 'I'll go,' she says. 'We're all done. Bye.'

'Bye,' Gwen says, softly.

I follow Rose a few steps from the bench, towards the house, and she turns in a quick movement and offers me her hand. I shake it. It's a fitting end to a business deal, and that's what this is. An exchange of information. I couldn't even claim to like Rose, with her devotion to her own illness when it could so easily be cured, and her certainty that some people deserve to die. But I'm prepared to accept that she is what life has made of her. Just as life is working its magic on me.

I'll never be totally true, unflinchingly loyal, to another friend again. Not even if I find one who I think deserves it. We are all unworthy of devotion that does not ask questions and demand answers before acting, and that is how it should be.

Gwen. Max. The Six. I should have asked questions of all of them.

'I'll keep the recordings safe,' says Rose. 'And in return you won't reveal to anyone where I am. Particularly if you go through with your idea.'

'Yes,' I say. 'That's fine.'

'You really want to do this?'

'I want to try.' Enough of funding films about the Stuck Six and other fairy tales. I'm going to use my money to make a film about Suscutin. A film that looks at the story from all angles. The kind of film Max might have made, if he'd not been given everything he ever wanted. I know Rose thinks they'll try and stop me. Personally, I think they won't care less. Everybody will still use their product anyway, even if it causes skin disease and death, and has its roots in other people's suffering.

Everybody except me. I haven't taken a Suscutin pill since that night at Rose's house. I'll moult sometime soon. I can feel it building.

I watch Rose leave, then take my seat next to Gwen, who says, 'My favourite duck is the one with the little white spot on his chest. See him? The other ducks never spend any time with him. I reckon he's an outcast.'

'You don't know a thing about him,' I say. 'He might be perfectly happy on his own. He might shun other duck company. He might not even realise he's a duck, and be wondering why he's sitting in a pond all day.'

'Fair enough.'

'Did she forgive you?'

'No, but she allowed me to ask for her forgiveness. That was the important bit. She let me ask. Can we go back inside now?'

She keeps refusing to use a wheelchair, so she leans heavily on me as we return to the big double doors of the hospice. 'So,' she says, when we're about halfway there, 'now you know me.'

'No, I don't. I don't know anybody,' I tell her. I take her weight, and keep on walking.

2011. **FROM THE OUTSIDE.**

The usual paparazzi were waiting for him, the three of them parked on the grass verge opposite the house, sitting separately in their cars, training their lenses upon him. Mik gave them a wave as he retrieved the shopping bag from the back seat. They didn't wave back, and that was usual too.

Grafham Water was choppy in the spring breeze, and Mik hadn't worn a coat to the supermarket. He hurried around the side of the house, and used the side door that led directly to the kitchen.

'Who's up for lunch?' he called.

Cheese, bread, salami, olives, lettuce, and a tin of tomato soup for Nicky who had been grouchy lately and needed comfort food: he had shopped to provide lunch options for everyone. He laid the purchases out on the counter, stacking Sunetra's timetable for night school and Howard's appointments diary to the side, then fetched six plates.

'Food,' he called, and the silence of the house struck him. 'Guys?'

He heard footsteps on the stairs, recognised Howard's heavy tread, and moved to meet him in the hallway.

'You'd better come upstairs,' Howard said.

'What's happening?'

'It's easier if you just come upstairs.'

He followed Howard to the largest of the bedrooms. The purple curtains Sunetra had made during a sudden sewing obsession were half-closed. Everyone was sitting on the king-sized bed, in a circle, and Nicky was at the head of the bed, cross-legged, in one of their shabby unisex robes with frayed sleeves.

'It just happened,' she said, and stretched out her arms to him. Dan and Liz shifted apart so he could reach her. As soon as he touched her, he knew what had taken place. Her skin was not the same. It felt so soft, so spongy. He felt immediate revulsion, but controlled the urge to pull away.

'It's okay,' she said. 'It came off cleanly. Really quick.'

Howard, still in the doorway, coughed once, twice, and then keened, high and long, covering his face with his hands. Dan got up from the bed and took him in his arms; Howard sobbed. His face, visible over Dan's shoulder, was horrifying. This is what great pain looks like, Mik thought. This is the terrible pain of loss. I will feel it too, just as soon as this numbness ends.

'It really is okay,' said Dan, to everyone, over Howard's head. 'This was always going to happen. We've talked about this. We'll stay together, won't we, for as long as we can.'

'Yes,' said Nicky. 'You don't get rid of me that easily.'

Sunetra leaned over to Liz, and stroked her hair. Mik fought against himself, made himself cradle Nicky, until the quality of sunlight through the gap in the curtain had changed, as time moved on.

Nicky patted his hand until he disengaged, then reached under one of the pillows and produced a folded white sheet. She shook it out upon the bed, and it took on human shape. She smoothed it out with her fingertips, using small, tentative movements.

'Here it is,' she said. 'Touch it.'

Sunetra, always so curious to have new experiences, placed her palm upon the ankle. She surprised Mik with a laugh, warm and deep and loud. Dan and Howard came closer, and touched it too, and then Liz, her hand trembling.

Mik, his eyes on their revelatory expressions, touched it and felt—

Love.

Love reflected. The love Nicky had felt for him, for them all, for what they had made together.

She had loved him perfectly. She had cherished him, believed in him, felt no jealousy or fear of his love in return. She had taken such delight in him.

He met her gaze. She was altering before him, moving away from love, rewriting herself and leaving him behind.

'Thank you,' he said. 'For having loved me like that.'

'You're welcome.'

What a gift love was. For a moment, as a memory, floating free from time and meaning. What a wonderful, willing gift.

'Did you call for lunch earlier?' said Nicky. 'I'm starving.' She got up from the bed and wandered from the room, while Howard started talking about keeping the skin safe and drawing up some sort of contract, an agreement to preserve all their skins for the future.

'To remind us of why we need to stay together, forever,' he said, as they ate, later.

ACKNOWLEDGEMENTS

Thank you to Dan Coxon, Helen Marshall, Mark Morris, Nina Allan, the Talking Cat, and the MNWers.

George Sandison liked the first half of this story, but told me there was a second half that still needed to be written. Thanks for being right, and for publishing it once it was (eventually) finished.

And thank you, Nick, Elsa and Barney.
I've got you all under my skin.

THE ARRIVAL OF MISSIVES

BY ALIYA WHITELEY

> "Stark, poetic, forthright and live with the numinous. One of the most original and haunting stories I have read in recent years."
> Nina Allan

☆ **2016 JOHN W. CAMPBELL AWARD FINALIST**
☆ **2017 BFS AWARDS FINALIST**
☆ **2016 BSFA AWARDS FNIALIST**
☆ **2016 JAMES TIPTREE JR. AWARD LONGLIST**
☆ **2017 SABOTEUR AWARDS SHORTLIST**

From Aliya Whiteley, author of the critically-acclaimed *The Beauty*, comes a genre-defying story of fate, free-will and the choices we make in life.

In the aftermath of the Great War, Shirley Fearn dreams of challenging the conventions of rural England, where life is as predictable as the changing of the seasons.

The scarred veteran Mr. Tiller, left disfigured by an impossible accident on the battlefields of France, brings with him a message: part prophecy, part warning. Will it prevent her mastering her own destiny?

Get a free extract

www.unsungstories.co.uk/trymissives

Follow Aliya  @AliyaWhiteley

OR SCAN THE QR CODE